Stitched Crosses

CRUSADE

a tale of AUDACIT'IN DOMINO in the High Middle Age

Joshua Rothe

GRAIL QUEST BOOKS ✢ BANGOR

PUBLISHER
Josh Radke

EDITOR
Joshua Anderson

COVER ILLUSTRATIONS
Paul Cox (front), Kasandra Radke (back)

A special thanks to Eric Postma.

STITCHED CROSSES: CRUSADE

PUBLICATION HISTORY
Paperback edition / July 2014
Revised edition / July 2015
ISBN: 978-0692256954

PRINTED IN THE UNITED STATES OF AMERICA
3 5 7 9 0 8 6 4 2

For information address:
Grail Quest Books
71 Broadway #3
Bangor, ME 04401

Grail Quest Books can be found online at
http://www.grailquestbooks.com

To the poor in spirit,
for theirs is the kingdom of heaven.

We therefore pray Thee,
  help Thy servants
    : whom Thou hast redeemed with
  Thy Precious blood.
Make them to be numbered
  with Thy Saints
    : in glory everlasting. ...

O Lord, have mercy upon us
  : have mercy upon us.

versicles from the 'Te Deum laudamus', 'HYMNUS SS.
AMBROSII ET AUGUSTINI', C. 3RD CENTURY (translation
from the BOOK OF COMMON PRAYER)

pRologue

By the time the last Roman legion to occupy the Britannia provinces were in Gaul coveting more Empire, a certain number of magistrates and officers were wed to Briton land, either in the flesh or in ambition: these desired to fight native enemies and Saxon invaders rather than the politics of the Caesars. And so the senior officers, under Constantine the Usurper, left the country to these men, that Roman civilisation might yet be immortal in this land of rain and rolling green.

    Some fell to the wars of the tribes, or political courts. Others, still burning for Rome, were crushed by the seeds of the Usurper: Uther and his son Arthur, the Pendragons. The defeated desired to be catechised, then Baptised into the death and rising of Christ, in accord with the earliest practices of the Church. They became privileged, some by their descendents, to preserve with great deeds that beautiful Realm Perelous, steeped in Christian enchantment—of which so few tales remain in the light of knowledge or belief.

Remembering the Sacred Grail of our LORD Jesus Christ, which passed from that Realm to dwell behind the veil of the Heavens, the blood of the sons of Old Logres grew staunch and unmoving in the kingdom that came to be Mercia.

More battles and more trials followed upon the land with the domination of the Saxon, but also peace and commerce painted the beauty of God's nature— for God was preached and believed in, pushing out the pagan shadows. And in the age called 'dark', still there was the Light of Heaven on Mercia and strong Christian lords rose to count their wealth of land and heirs to be God's blessing.

One such lord was Markus, second so-named after his forefather of five removed generations, who was descended from one of the lesser officers of Rome to stay and chance his lot with the Britons with whom he mixed. Markus held close council with Offa of Thingfrith, supporting his cause against Beornred, who took Mercia for himself after the murder of his king—the faithless Æthelbald (who once defied even Boniface, the Blessed Apostle of Germania).

When the war was ended and Offa the Mighty upon the Mercian throne, Markus, now also called 'the Fearless', was given a lordship in the north of the kingdom, to act as sentinel upon Northumbria. Wielding his storied blade, Audacit'in-Domino, this lordship he and his descendents defended against the Saxons of Wessex and Odin's sons from across the North Sea.

Later, Offred, the Lord of Audaciter-Deus in the age when several peoples coveted the lands of Britain, was counted amongst the alliance of men that routed the Norse invaders for the last time. But their victory was ill-timed for one named William, of the House of Normandy, was arrived to forever shift the course of the great island of the Britons.

The Normans took the lands of many lords and made war on those few remaining who did not bow before their Norman overseers—of which those of Saxon origin were chief. Before an alliance could be forged among those resisting their overlords, the Church hoped to stop the warring afflicting all Western Christendom by turning the focus to giving an answer to those waging war in the name of Allah: the Moors who came to occupy Iberia and nearly all of the Kingdom of the Franks (if not for the heroic deeds of the grandfather of Charlemagne), and the Saracens who would usurp the whole land where Christ had walked, died, arisen and ascended. To prevent this end many sons of nobles came to join the Order of the Poor Knights of the Temple; those who had no great claim or heraldry, and yet would be knightly warriors for Christendom, came to the Order of the Hospital of Saint John the Baptist. By way of service to these Orders, the Church did hope to end the long years of bloodshed and raise up new nobilities where rivalries were cold and lords would remember Whom they owed their service.

And there was a Saxon lord by name of

Edelstan, four generations from Offred, who did sire a daughter named Dawnlyn, because Lord Edelstan thought of her as a rising hope to her people. Also he had a son whom he gave the name Markus, in honour of the great fathers of Audaciter-Deus, for he did intend that his son would preserve the lineage in the faith with noble service to the House.

Alas, Lord Edelstan and his Lady were slain in a secret raid, of which the origin was never determined; this was in the waning summer, two years after granting a begrudging blessing to their son to go to Templecombe for his training to be a Knight Templar. The young lord did hope that his being dedicated to the Holy Order would provide leverage against further molestation of his Saxon House if the oppressors truly be of Christian heart.

With the death of the Lord and his wife, and Markus away to make war upon the enemies of the Church, Dawnlyn became Lady of Audaciter-Deus. She was tall in stature and wise in her councils, and all were thwarted in their secret efforts to overthrow the Saxon House of that land. Thus Audaciter-Deus gave courage to the Saxon nobles and it was oft used as a place of secret meetings and plannings—although the Lady was increasingly known to discourage rebellion and support the rule of the House of Plantagenet in order to best preserve the Saxon lines.

For long years there were no tidings of the Son of Edelstan to Audaciter-Deus Hall so that it seemed to Lady Dawnlyn that she were the last of her long line. Yet she courted hope with each sunrise for she could not despair a death that was not yet revealed; and her faith in God was strong and fruitful.

One moon-filled night, a knock stirred the hall. A Christian knight of the House of Ibelin, accompanied by a woman of simple beauty (whom the Lady did recognise from her childhood) stood in the arch; behind them was a litter bearing the limp—but alive—form of the young Lord of Audaciter-Deus.

When Markus was laid in his bed and inspected by his sister a furrow of confusion did cross her face. Turning to the Knight: "His wounds are not grave and indeed well tended, sir Knight. Why then does he appear as one upon the threshold of death?"

The Knight looked upon Dawnlyn with foreknowledge of the question. "The grave wound is beyond the skill of a physician, milady, for the injury is in the mind and not upon the body. If you would have his recovery then patient love and fervent prayer are the best medicines."

"Of those remedies there are plenty within these borders." The Lady turned back to her brother. "Thus, he *shall* return to us whole." And she thanked the Knight for his kindness and skill, giving him food and quarter for as long as he dwelled in Audaciter-Deus.

I: a man called

The Holy City of God belonged to the banners of Allah. Early in the eighty-seventh autumn of the second century and millennial after the Blessed Incarnation of God as Jesus the Christ, Jerusalem bowed its great head to the Saracen champion and Sultan of Egypt, *Salah ad-Din Yusuf Ibn Ayyub*: Saladin.

With his occupation of the city, many Christians no longer heard the Voice of God in *Outremer*—the kingdom of Christian states in the Holy Land of the LORD. A myriad thought fondly once again of the great shores of the West, and longed to return; a portion of those were a great many Knights, including a some of the Blessed Orders of the Temple and Saint John the Baptist. These were indeed few, as it burned in the hearts of these bearers of the Red and White Crosses—stitched with fidelity upon their breasts—to retake the Sacred City where Christ poured forth his lifeblood for the salvation of the world.

And so, like the bear in hibernation, these

Knights of the Cross waited for the sweet smell of reprisal's spring.

It can only be guessed that those of the Blessed Orders that did lay eyes again on the shores and horizons of Western Christendom did so for only the most personal of intent and shortest of time; at the least to return to the kingdom without its Crowning Jewel with some measure of renewed strength, to wage what most piously believed to be a righteous war on behalf of the *Ecclesia Militans*—a war begun by the Muslim when they marched into Damascus, then Jerusalem some six centuries prior; when North Africa and Iberia were overrun, and nearly all the West if Charles, called 'the Hammer', had not stopped Abderame at Tours; when Sicily was occupied, then Benevento; when the *Status Pontificius* was sacked and *Basilica Sancti Petri* looted like a common chest. All well before the first millennium *Anno Domini* had set upon the horizon.

But these politics and rivalries were not presently on the mind of the Hospitaller Knight as he made his way upon a forested road in that part of Norman Britain called —shire. Not many of England's sons had taken up the Cross, for many were needed to keep the balance of Anglo-Saxon and Scot against the Norman. Indeed the lords of these Houses at first applauded the news of the warrior pilgrimages to the East as they looked to accomplish sword-work against the more local Norman infidel. But the idea to glorify Holy God, by freeing the East from the rule of the Saracen, was too strong a wine from which to yield for the promising young princes of Ivanhoe, Dunkeld, and Audaciter-Deus.

A wind blew through the bare trees, forcing a violent shiver. The Knight was used to the hot breath of the desert. It had been years since the kiss of a Christian winter last touched his beardless face.

Ahead the Hospitaller saw a form close to passing him on the road. "Hallo, yonder Christian!" he called forth in the harsh accent of Eastphalia.

"And God be with'ye," came a gruff, yet amicable, voice.

When the Hospitaller reached the spot where the traveller tarried he said, "If you would be so kind as to help a knight of Christ."

"Would be but a blessing, sir Knight. How may I be of service?"

The Hospitaller nodded. "I seek the property of the Lady of this region. Is this the road?"

"Aye, this very one, sir Knight. But the Lady of Audaciter-Deus is not available for audience, as I hear it. Her brother is about if it pleases you."

The traveller's countenance shifted to one like pity and he rubbed his chin. His voice was noticeably lower.

"Is there more, friend?"

"You would have more speed getting one of these lonely trees to talk than the lord of this shire, I'm afraid. Keep your sword close; he is a brooding type and much more given to acceptin' a strange face as Norman, be he in truth or not"

The Hospitaller nodded again. "Thanks to you, good sir. A blessing for your helpful conversation, and good counsel." The Knight wasted no time moving his horse forward.

"You'll find him returning from the smithy soon," the Knight heard the peasant call after him through the frigid breeze.

The Hospitaller soon learned the peasant could not have been more correct. For just as his mount crested the hill, he could discern a distant figure making his way along a footpath from a building belching black smoke from its chimney.

A small cottage beckoned not half a stone's throw from where the mounted Knight now stood dismounted. A servant girl came out to meet the Hospitaller. She motioned to take his horse and he nodded in gratitude.

When the steed had been tied to a stall and given some straw, the young girl led the Hospitaller across the way to the cottage. Inside the homely structure, she silently served him a draught of water and a plate with bread and a bone stick of fowl. Then she bowed and made her departure saying only, "My master will join your supper in his time."

The Hospitaller did not know how long he would be waiting, but judging by the similar plate of food on a small table near the fire it would not be long. The Knight took his fare to that table and surveyed the structure. It was one room; a cot located in the corner was heaped with fabrics and a few empty baskets, so the Hospitaller concluded that the cottage was used mostly for refreshment and receiving unsolicited guests. Close to the gate, it was the ideal place for the Knight to transact his short business.

The Hospitaller knew little of the one who would soon be his host. The hard-won facts at his disposal confirmed the lord of this shire as being in Outremer before Saladin's occupation. His business, and the length of his stay, remained a mystery. Despite the scarcity of information, the Hospitaller would know if his host and the Templar he sought were one and the same.

The Knight of The Baptist took another hearty bite of his roll of bread; on the second swallow of his drink, the door burst open. The man that clambered through the door was not heavy-set, but he could certainly turn the tide of a fight he meant to win. The drawn sword in his hand indicated that a fight in the present was not out of the question.

"Are you the Knight of the Hospital that was given admittance?" The man's voice was a clear baritone and one to which men desiring a leader would gladly listen.

The Hospitaller looked into the man's eyes. They reflected a kindled fire but revealed no sign of unprovoked violent intent. Finally he nodded to the swordsman. "I am, sir, and you, I presume, are the lord of this blessed land."

The man returned the nod with the hint of

a snarl. "It is dangerous to conceal the markings of your Order, Knight. Suppose I considered you a Norman?"

"I supposed you would consider my sword resting not a breath away from you."

The man followed the Hospitaller's gaze to the featureless sword that was indeed lying upon a bench, sheathed.

The shire-lord looked back to the Knight. "Normans do not need swords to kill their marks." He replaced his princely blade within its cover. "What business have you here?"

"I seek Sir Honour the Templar. He is said to be the brother of the Lady of this estate."

Markus stared hard at the Hospitaller and long enough for awkward discomfort to make itself an unwanted guest for the duration. Without answering the assertion put forth, the shire-lord ambled to the table. Never taking his eyes from the Hospitaller, he dropped himself into the chair across from the Knight and proceeded to chew on a crust of bread.

When he had dispensed of the bread, and taken several long draughts of water, he leaned back in his chair and regarded the Hospitaller for long beats. "The Lady has but one brother," he said evenly, "and he sits before you now. No man by name of 'Honour' dwells here."

Even in the dim light, the Hospitaller could discern the permanently darkened skin behind the lord's black-bearded face, which could only be achieved by long service in a baking wilderness. The eyes gave away no signs of mal-deception. But the man's appearance was good enough for Saint John's Knight to press the matter.

"Good sir, I do empathize with the precaution of hiding your identity. I assure you that my intentions are neither to uproot you, nor are they in league with the Norman brutes whose want it is to possess this land." The Hospitaller saw that Markus would allow him to continue a bit longer. "I have broken from the duties of the White Cross to but bring one message to Sir Honour of the Templar Order;" the Knight produced a small scroll from beneath his black mantle, "one in the hand of a mutual friend."

The Lord of Audaciter-Deus continued to stare in silence at the Knight, perhaps hoping the flicker of the flame against his features might conjure an unnatural fear in the Hospitaller resulting in a want to depart, in haste. But the Hospitaller held fast the unfriendly gaze.

"Say the name of this 'friend'. I shall judge if it be a mutual companion, or the tidings of a new enemy."

"Are you Sir Honour then?"

"I am called Markus—the third so-named in the line of this House. Concerning the one you seek: I may know of him. And if I do then I will also know of his friends, for I either know a man completely or not at all. That must suffice for your person; or you can hold your message for ears you deem more worthy."

The Hospitaller found he had little leverage: at worst the man would deny knowledge of the name, likely forgetting it as just another name among men—which is exactly what it was, save for those who had been in the message-writer's fellowship.

"Brother Percy; a knight who belonged to the same Order of Cross you see before you now." The Hospitaller detected a twitch of the man's lip. "Does your silence acquit my persistance, sir?"

"You speak of this mutual friend as if he be evermore with Holy God," Markus answered.

The Hospitaller looked down, hoping to bury the lump in his throat, for the pain in his heart was still unhealed. "Indeed; good Sir Percy took a golden chariot at Hattin, along with many a good Christian knight and soldier."

Markus got up with such fierceness that his chair tumbled back a couple paces to the floor. He looked like a man trying to keep his sanity after his first taste of battle. Heavy breaths passed his lips, and something about the noble perishing whilst the ignoble lingered.

When it seemed the Saxon lord's composure had sufficiently returned, the Hospitaller risked his question again. "Are you then Sir Honour, for whom this message is intended?"

Markus swallowed, and answered low and even. "The name you seek is here but the one to whom it once belonged is but a shadow. Even so, if I must don the mantle of 'Sir Honour' to hear the words of good Percy then it is a burden I will bear with gladness for this brief occasion."

The Hospitaller nodded and set the sealed scroll on the table before the Templar as he gathered his chair and sat upon it again. He glared at the rolled parchment as if he could ascertain the contents by his steely gaze alone.

When he took the note into his hands, he seemed barely to want to touch it out of fear that even the lightest of contact might crumble the note to dust. He inspected the seal, then replaced the scroll on the table between them. "You know its contents," he said.

"I do," the Hospitaller agreed. "It accompanied another sealed letter addressed to me. Percy requested that I commit the words on the parchment before us to memory, lest the note be lost or require destruction."

Markus indicated the hearth with his thumb. "This message may as well be in that fire."

The Knight looked at Markus with concern. "You have lost the language of the Church?"

"The words of the Holy Father and his council have brought me much death and regret," Markus said. "I retain Christian Latin for hearing, to receive the Sacred Mass, but I have no need to corrupt my eyes and tongue. It has been this way since... since before Hattin. Good Percy knew this; thus either Holy God has ceased his favor upon you or your presence is the tidings of ill events." Markus rose, unsheathing his sword.

The Hospitaller did not like this turn of events. "Open the letter, sir. Let me read you his words..." he said in as calm and serious a tone as he could. He remained in his seat, hoping the Saxon prince would see this and conclude the Knight to be harmless.

The Knight's air of calm and lack of action was lost on the Lord of Audaciter-Deus; he approached with the sureness of a stoic warrior. "One who trusts a tame animal just come in from the wild, should expect to lose their hand."

"I beg you to open the letter, good sir," the Hospitaller repeated, with a hint of concern beginning to creep into his tone.

"A prayer of salvation would be a better choice of words, spy," came the retort.

The Knight now understood the pressing situation with alarming clarity. "You think me a Norman agent?"

Markus slowed his advance. "Or of the Papal court. I will not be told that I am destined for Jerusalem for the salvation of my kin or my soul. This I am undertaking, in my country, until my death." He stopped, as if halted by some invisible barrier, then ambled forward again. "If not for the last 'holy pilgrimage', I would not have the worst of all sins to atone. I fear that not a hundred lifetimes will be enough to appease Heaven for the stain on my heart. But sending one of Rome's messengers to our Highest Judge to answer for the *magna Curia* might save me from the hottest of hell's fires."

As Markus spoke, the Hospitaller had gotten hold of the note, and worked hastily to release the seal. But time was no longer his ally. The glint of the Saxon's blade bent a ray of the setting sun off its edge as Markus raised it above him for a mighty strike. Just then the Hospitaller's finger slid beneath the wax, releasing the letter from its rolled state.

Markus's foot lashed out, striking the seat of the chair and tipping it and its occupant straight backward. But as he fell, the Knight thrust the parchment into the air.

The breaths of the two men and the cracks of the fire filled the tense moments of inaction. The muscles of Markus's arms tensed as he held his weapon aloft and gazed upon the empty note before him—empty save the sign of Sir Percy clearly drawn upon the paper as proof the Hospitaller's words were genuine.

Seeing the imminence of his doom retreating, the Hospitaller said, "Indeed our brother knew you of your choice to become mute and blind. This he explained as the necessary reason for why I had to commit his message to you solely to mind."

Markus lowered his sword, threw it upon the table. "Father in Heaven why must you burden an ass already approaching the cliff!" he cried aloud.

The Knight's heart wrenched at the appeal for mercy. He regained his feet and placed a hand on the shoulder of the Saxon lord. "Let not your attack on my person disrupt your peace. Of all your time with our Percy, did he not remind you that a heavy heart which need not be heavy troubles God as much as any transgression?"

Markus turned his gaze to look upon the Hospitaller, but the man had taken little hope from the absolution. The hint of a smile flashed briefly across the young Lord's lips. "Perhaps God desires to save me after all," he said with a nod. "What name have you?"

"I am called Charle."

Markus picked up his sword: Charle noticed it had two small inset Crosses on either end of the cross-guard, a third, larger, was set within the pommel—all three were comprised of gold; there was writing along the guard and fuller of which the Hospitaller could not make out. "And where is your true and honourable blade?"

Charle indicated a place beside the entrance. "I put it there upon the bench, so as not to unsettle the servant girl."

Markus looked at Charle briefly. "That was no servant girl. Her name is Mairín and she is a free lady on these lands as if she was my kin."

"I beg your forgiveness, Sir Honour."

"I will not judge ignorance," Markus replied evenly. "And please, call me Markus. 'Sir Honour the Templar' perished with the rest of Christian hope for Outremer at Hattin.

He walked to the bench and placed his sword

beside that of his guest's: "Now if I should find reason to lose my wits again, you will have the fair chance to separate them from this body." The moment, meant to be filled by the brief exhale of a laugh or some other manner of lightening the air, instead remained discomfited between the two weary Knights.

The lord ambled across the room, back to his place across from Charle. "So, what of this message from our brother, Hospitaller?"

"In brief," Charle replied around a crust of bread, "Percy left a 'token of great value' to you at the Church marking the Most Holy Resurrection of our LORD Christ." Charle reached beneath his cloak. "The item—"

Markus sucked in a breath, loosed it again saturated with contempt, and dug a finger into the grain of the table. "Percy and his riddles."

The forehead of the Hospitaller creased; he removed his hand from whatever he meant to retrieve. "Why do you perceive a mystery?"

Markus looked from beneath his cloak of irritation. "Brother Knight, we soldiers of the Cross are hardly allowed more than battle to help digest our food and fray our clothes. Along with our Creator, we share these *common* elements. There is nothing that Percy would have possessed of mine that was not also his, and of *equal* importance. If there was one thing we did not have in common it was his love of playful ambiguity. More than once I was witness to him sending a man on a road with little more than a proverb and God's blessing. If they returned it was red-faced and ready to cuff our blessed Percy for sending them on a road that yielded little more than soulful reflection and sunburn."

Charle watched him.

"Are you very sure this is all Percy intended for you?" the Hospitaller asked finally.

"As sure as God's righteous Judgment," Markus responded.

"So his purpose could not have been to compel these men to walk with their Lord a spell? Possibly to embrace penance in preparation of Mass? Or to simply appreciate the land, the people for which they fought, the good Providence from the LORD of Heaven?"

Charle waited for a response from his host, but none was forthcoming.

"Very well, Markus. The 'common element' of 'equal importance' awaits you at the Most Holy Sepulchre of our Lord Jesus Christ."

The Saxon prince was immediately defensive. "You spoke that your intentions were not to uproot me, Hospitaller! I find it beyond curious that your presence so conveniently parallels that of the call by King Richard of England to form an army to liberate Jerusalem."

The Hospitaller bowed and raised his head amicably, but his words were as darts. "A pardon for my lack of clarity. My hope that you would have stayed in this land remains. It is the words of *Percy* which confirms your road and the king's are the same, even though your purposes are not."

Markus turned to the hearth. For long minutes he stood there, losing himself to the rhythm of the fire as Charle watched him. He could imagine the conversations Percy must have had with this Templar, and he could picture Percy liking this young lord very much. Percy never made a man into something he was not; he took each of God's creatures as they were and sent them on paths he felt they needed to walk, that God might do His Work upon them.

"How will you traverse the pilgrim road set before you, Markus?" Charle pressed.

Markus would not be intimidated. "At present I must remain here until my sister returns."

"And after?" Charle did not enjoy it, to push, but he knew Percy would have; there was much at stake.

"With Richard leaving I think it best if I remain here. My father liked Richard; he was convinced that for all the Plantaget's foibles he was fair, and was owed our loyalty. But our good king is too little in his kingdom. This breeds enemies, lawlessness, injustice..."

"But Percy—"

Markus turned from the hearth with ferocity: "No one loved our brother more than I, Charle. But Percy was not a man with family, or land seen as ripe for plucking."

"Knights of our Order take oaths, severing us

from that which would bond us to this world."

"Gaze upon my chest, Hospitaller! Do you see a Cross of Red or White stitch upon its landscape?"

"Even without oath, men are warned by Christ to make no thing equal or above the LORD, Who is our salvation. Surely the well-being of the soul entrusted to you is considered before family, country, and the security of one's temporal holdings." Charle noted that the hearth was not responsible for the flame now kindled in the eyes of the Templar.

"I have freely given myself and the resources of this land to the service of God, Church, and man, Charle; I will not have my loyalty or love of God questioned! If God desires me upon the road you have made known to me then I shall be turned upon it as did God to Blessed Jonah!"

Nothing further concerning the matter at hand passed between them, and both used the time to consider what to do next.

It was Markus who finally spoke, in an even tone that might be considered friendly on another day. "Do you have lodging for the night, Charle?"

The Hospitaller indicated that he did not; "... if it is convenient for you." .

"Hospitality is not offered on this blessed land with the consideration of convenience. Consider this House your home."

"You are gracious, sir. My stay must be brief as I am to be in Brittany before the moon is full."

Markus nodded. "You will have full provision

for yourself and horse when you see fit to depart."

"Blessings on this house," Charle replied after he had retrieved his sword. Then he departed, perceiving the Lord of Audaciter-Deus watched after him, even long after the he had disappeared into the deep shadows of twilight.

II : long understandings

The fire in the broad hearth of the practical quarters of Markus, son of Edelstan, cracked and whined. It had been the only sound for the last hour, and its warmth was more than sufficient for the body. But Markus could not feed the flame enough to fight off the unnatural chill that clung to his bones. Upon a chair, he smoked a crude hand-made pipe and glared at the woven tunic sitting upon a coffer across the room; the Red Cross upon the chest shown brilliant in the blazing light.

The latch on the door lifted and fell. Markus got up quickly, moving in haste to the chest. "Come," he said. By the time the door opened, he sat upon the edge of the box, the tunic sufficiently in his shadow.

Mairín presented herself plainly (as usual): a simple full-length dress of canary blue with a pattern of deeper blue swirling from shoulder to shoulder across the modest front. In her hands were clean blankets topped by a pouch of tobacco and fresh pieces of shortbread.

"And how is our guest?" Markus wondered aloud when the door latched behind her.

Mairín placed the items onto a small table near the fireplace. "He accepted only the necessities," she responded.

Charle was a member of a Blessed Order, as Markus had once been. Of course he would deny all comforts not allowed by his station. Markus had always enjoyed the presence of the brothers of the Baptist saint. They were a Godly group of servants— excellent manners, skilled healers, clear wisdom, and deadly enough to any who would oppose them un-mounted.

Markus saw Mairín moving to exit, clearly interpreting Markus's silence as a desire to be left alone. Or perhaps she had come for a different reason (at the behest of Charle to convince him of his duty?) and now thought the better of it.

"What is on your mind, milady?"

She paused, her back facing him, probably to help gain composure— "Why does a Knight of Christ hesitate to set foot upon a road laid before him?"

So she had heard the conversation, or been made privy to its basic nature. Mairín was not the prying type, so perhaps this knowledge she bore was the will of God. Or perhaps she was speaking in the context of lingering pain from an adolescent conversation long ago, when he showed no hesitance towards the East after her professed love to him.

"What could be in Jerusalem that I do not already have here?"

"I know that you are distressed, milord. And it is said that Jerusalem can heal this; perhaps what is awaiting you there even moreso."

"Ah." Markus took a long draw on his pipe. "Well, at present the Saracen controls its sacred walls. Only a Christian who is expired, or very wealthy, is given leave to pass safely through its great gates." Markus settled himself upon the chest behind him. "And good Percy was less than clear as to what awaits me in the blessed Church of the Sepulchre—a sanctuary that was reduced to ruin the last time its enemies took the city. Am I to brave all these things on a whim, for some trinket shackled to a dead man's wisdom in a place that assuredly no longer exists in this world to serve men?"

She turned to face him now. "Even so, God has charged you there."

Now Markus wondered if she was trying to rid herself of his person, so the memory would wane to nothing, as a wisp of smoke from an extinguished candle. "God, or the Church?"

She turned to him with a resoluteness in her eyes and posture that made Markus's heart leap. "Are they not the same?"

Were they? Certainly in the early centuries following Christ and his disciples; like water on parched soil did the words of Ignatius, Clement, Polycarp, and Athanasius water the soul. But Charlemagne, in his efforts to govern the vast Kingdom of the Franks, fed dangerous fuel to the gorging fire-tempest that is the depravity conceived in every womb: his political manoeuvrings birthed lies and damaging rivalries, as much in the blessed sanctuaries as in the royal courts.

In the time that Markus had spent in the East, the things he had experienced as 'Sir Honour' were indicative of a Church ever more falling to the temptation of invoking the Divine to legitimize thrones (thus receiving immense tithes and reciprocal favours in ecclesiastical appointments); those counselling God-inspired wisdom in government and servanthood were finding a tougher audience. The perceived behaviour of the bishops and princes spoke well to the born nature excited to kill for its own sake, to the iniquitous flesh oft-revolted by repentance. Such lawlessness overtook some of his own Templar brothers, convinced none would condemn such elite fighting men; eschewing rebuke they falsely believed the promise of absolution was assured, without condition or the pain of humility, to 'holy Knights'.

Despite all this, Markus had found that faith and penitence weighed upon the spirits of most of his fellows and the soldiers with whom he and his Order served daily. They appreciated the solemnity of their task to guard the Church, without thought of gain, dedicating their service with sincerity to the glory of Christ—like the chivalric warriors Gawain and Perceval (and others of Arthur's court), Roland the Frank, and the Cid of Iberia, recounted so often through story and song. Thirsting for righteousness in the sight of Heaven, beneath the Cross of their salvation, these decent men embraced the preaching of Urban II (and the popes thereafter) that they would be relieved of all penance for their sins while they selflessly preserved the Christian kingdoms and defended pilgrims upon their pious journeys.

Markus, with all Christendom, agreed: the Saracen armies needed to be checked, the holy places protected from their hateful destructiveness. But there was something missing in the way the Church preached on this good work; the notion that one could make war in exchange for spiritual mercy had been fiercely debated ahead of Urban's controversial speech at Claremont. Simple belief in Christ had become lost inside the great fortress of the Holy See: 'right-action' meant keeping alive Church traditions and rules without question; severe 'miscreants' were reprimanded, or even excommunicated, in the hope judgment on a few would keep the many in line to serve the uneasy peace among the realms and the ambitions of the papal *Curia*. Markus recalled being taught by his captain of Jesus rebuking the Jews for giving equal—even higher—value to the fallible laws of religious councils over the *salvificus* exhortations of God through the Prophets, for shaping their spiritual identity around foundations of sand instead of their distinctive character as 'God's people, mercifully chosen, to bear witness' as 'living stones built upon the Capstone, that is Christ.'

"Milord...?"

Markus looked into the enquiring eyes of Mairín.

"Are you alright, milord?"

"Yes…" Markus broke his gaze and rose from the chest to stand before the fire. He needed to answer her; there was no reason to allow the devil to cause harm to a precious soul by doubting every brother, sister, shepherd in the Church. "One must be always vigilant—even if the Church were wholly led by the most honourable of men. It seems we are presently like the Jews long past: beneath the rule of one 'King Saul' after another." An appearance of concern was waxing over the face of the young lady. "Be assured, Mairín: God is most certainly among us, affirming His promises through a great many of His ordained; the Bride of Christ still basks in the Light of His Sacramental Mysteries, and the Nicene Confession. My wariness comes from a suspicion that men of influence, notably in the Papal Court, seek my presence, perhaps for ill intent." He paused: how much should he say? Was he revealing perilous details for the sake she would disassociate from him? "My captain in Outremer was sought for much counsel. He became a known critic of the waning Godly wisdom of certain over-lords and knights; also the Curia's capriciousness in matters of spiritual well-being in the kingdom beyond relief from penance for bearing arms against the Saracen." Markus took a deep breath, and unthreaded his anxious fingers. "I agreed on many of these matters, perhaps too openly. Yet his was not a shrill voice, lest disunity compromise us in battle; it was not our desire to create division but a beacon that would compel men to look again on the light of Christ. But not all saw it as so..."

"I wish I could have met your captain, milord."

Markus pressed his lips and let a the hint of smile deliver the message of his appreciation.

"So you think the Hospitaller ignoble," she continued, "and thus his message that you are to go to Jerusalem."

"No. Charle is as true as they come within that Order. But God does not speak only through Blessed Knights."

Mairín raised her face again. "But how can you know?"

Her question carried no disrespect, indeed it was proof of time well spent in the presence of his sister. Even so it resulted quickly in a scowl that reflected the frustration she could not see roiling within the Saxon prince. "Truly; I will be praying on it, milady."

The dimming of Mairín's face spoke to her unhappiness at Markus's response. His demeanour faded with hers: she had come to know him well, for she was likely concluding it was *un*likely he would ever return to Jerusalem.

Markus could not say 'never': he had to remain open to God's calling, but he allowed his silence on the details of the decision to carry the weight of the verdict to the woman before him, and to the Hospitaller if she felt compelled to answer his inquiries. And yet... "You believe I am called to the City of the Passion of our LORD Christ?"

Mairín was taken by surprise, as expected. She could not know that the query was partly intended for Heaven. Her answer would do much to confirm or deny the Hospitaller's suggestion that God wanted him back in Outremer. Markus had been so confident in rebuking the Knight's suggestion. So why did his heart pick up its pace as he waited for her answer?

Mairín was careful in her response. "I cannot reason in this moment why you should—"

Shouts echoed from a nearby stair, followed quickly by running feet.

A guard pounded on the door frantically: "Lord Markus: We are breached, in the—!" The voice was drowned by the crashing of metal.

Markus retrieved Audacit'in-Domino—the blade of his House—with the disciplined haste he was taught. He backed Mairín with his hand to the side of the fireplace that was most out of sight. "Stay here." He fixed onto her eyes for confirmation that she agreed to what he was telling her. Only when he received it did he break the glare and run for the door.

The corridor side of the threshold revealed three swords for every one, favouring the invaders in this part of the battle. Markus reduced those odds with a quick thrust of his sword into the lower back of an attacker in the wrong place for his skirmish. Markus stepped into the corridor, reflexed back into his quarters and regarded for a moment the two shafts now buried in the door; Providence had saved him from catching a shaft both in his crown and throat. The guard he had just saved had not been so blessed.

A stranger ran past; Markus struck the man in the back of the head with the flat of his small axe. The enemy stumbled forward, but caught his feet and swung around with a one-handed, off-balance reverse strike with his sword. The move was easy enough to dodge and it left the opponent with a vulnerable torso. One two-handed counter-strike left the man face-first on the ground, perhaps to contemplate his reckless attack in his final minutes.

Markus rounded the corner and immediately realized his mistake. A new enemy raked his weapon across Markus's stomach. It was a short-sword, sparing Markus from a wound worse than one requiring several turns of a surgeon's thread. The trespasser curled a lip and Markus watched the man's eyes searching for the best move: a swift hack was chosen, followed by another, then an uncreative vertical slash. The man was hiding fatigue, so Markus jabbed four times, made a high cut motion catching the foe squarely in the mouth with one end of the crossguard of his sword. The intruder wouldn't feel the grisly results for a couple hours: he lay on the ground unconscious; the injury would be useful during interrogation.

Markus leaned on the wall to catch his breath

and assess the gash on his stomach. A scream—
Mairín's scream—snapped his eyes to the direction
of his quarters. Images from the time he left the room
were conjured by his mind as he rushed back: a second
invader had rushed past him when he had been taken
by surprise rounding the corner. He cursed himself
for being so mindless as he limped-ran.

A terrible scene framed itself in the doorway:
Mairín, struggling desperately against an enemy that
intended base debauchery in the way he gripped her.

"Unhand her, devil's pawn." Markus entered
the room readied for a fight.

The villain turned on a coin with his swordarm
in such a deft maneuver that the man's blade took
Markus's clear out of his hand; the weapon landed
somewhere on the ground nearby. He made no move
to retrieve it: Mairín had used the split seconds of
freedom to wield the poker tool in her hand with
superb ferocity. The defiler stumbled back towards
the fireplace, reflexively halting his descent with a
free hand against the stones. Mairín used the fresh
moment of vulnerability to strike the man across the
neck, turning him to fall face first into the hellish
blaze. Markus engulfed the dear woman, to mute the
inhuman scream from the thrashing, aflame body as
he rushed her to safety up the corridor. A row of
his own sentries stood about one hundred fifty feet
ahead—facing away, disconnected from where the
battle seemed to be moving.

No: six of the guards fell nearly in unison,

revealing a single-file wall of archers partially hid by the shadows. He turned immediately, placing Mairín in front of himself.

"*Salvo!*"

The seconds crawled to minutes in the estimation of his mind as he juked and ducked the shafts that flew past them: a tip grazed his thigh, another ripped fabric from Mairín's robin's egg coloured dress. They rounded the corner—

Waiting for them was a lone archer. Markus knew he was dead-spotted in the invader's sights. The only thought in his head was *Me.* He felt the shaft settle deep in his shoulder. The archer was poised for a second shot, then he collapsed—ambushed by someone behind. Markus turned away, thinking he could retreat to his quarters and protect Mairín there before the pain grew unbearable. But the battle had returned to the passageways. Even now a duel blocked their path.

The blurred vision foretold that Markus was about to become null for the remainder of this fight. He started to pitch forward, then felt his weight carry him violently backwards.

A White Cross blazed in his eyes.

Then there was nothing.

†　†　†

The heat that fell around Markus was immeasurable. Through the orange wall that circled him he could hear the agonized cries of men and steel on steel. But he could not seem to penetrate the thickness about him. The sound of horses' hooves to his left caught his attention. Markus drew his sword. Almost immediately, the wall of flame parted and Markus could see the golden True Cross before him. Markus ran to his charge but the Cross got no nearer. The flames ran before him on either side, and yet the great relic remained on the horizon...possibly even further away than when he first saw it. Markus was overtaken by men—Christian Knights from the Hospitallers, the Jerusalem army, and his own Order, the Templars. They all ran towards the Cross, or was it towards the Muslim forces now surrounding the cherished artefact? Panic struck Markus in the chest like a shield blow. The enemy were too many. Markus tried to get the Knights to halt. The heat intensified and the men of Christendom began to wilt like plants in the oppressive atmosphere. They fell singly at first, then by the dozens, and then by the hundreds. Markus overtook them in quick pace, pausing only briefly to gaze into their blank stares and twisted, parched lips. The heat was stifling now and the corpses turned red as steel cooling from the furnace; their garments disappeared in the intense heat and their flesh melted into pools of gore. Markus saw he was holding a bucket of water and he quickly poured the cool liquid over the bodies. But the water evaporated before it even came close to the gaping mouths. Markus reached out to steady a man about to collapse nearby and heard the hissing of his own flesh burning as it touched the mail coif of the Knight. Then by the miracle of Holy God, a shadow stretched over the gruesome scene. Markus turned and saw the True Cross as the source of the blessed shade. Just as it reached his feet, the shadow suddenly retreated: the Cross was falling. The Saracen cavalry pulled long ropes from their horses. Into the sand the army descended, pulling the Cross of Christ with them. In a moment Markus was alone with a fierce wind; the heat faded and the mass of bones joined the gale as dust. Despite that he believed the storm would carry him away at any moment, Markus peered at the spot where he had seen the Cross of his Saviour sink. Frantically he clawed at the ground. He could save the Cross, he could feel it. And there it was! He felt its rigid form scrape his fingers. His muscles screaming, he thrust his hands deep into the sand until both elbows disappeared into the grains. He took a firm grip of the centre beam and pulled. He prayed for strength and new life entered his body. The Cross became like a feather. And then Markus was on his back. He could feel the beautiful weight of the Cross on his chest. For a moment he collected his breath. Then he opened his eyes to embrace the wondrous mark of his faith—No! The sacred golden form did not meet his eyes. But the empty sockets of Percy did! Markus dug his heels into the sand, pushing himself from beneath the body. A great Light dawned on the eastern horizon...a Holy Light. It grew nearer. A severe panic stole Markus's breath and he dug in his heels again. His mind raged in battle against his rapid heartbeat. Why was he running from the Light? His heels no longer gave him traction. Markus saw a rope noosed about his foot. He followed the line to where it looped around the top of the golden vertical beam of the True Cross. It was like moving against a mountain, and still the Light came from the hill far ahead. Markus knew it to be the Purity of the King of Kings. It was a Light he had no right to enter. Its Righteous Presence was more damning than the Cross. Markus craved the Light, and hated it far beyond any emotion aimed at an enemy. As Markus lay in the shadow of the Cross, The Light offered him peace but judged him absolutely unworthy: His guilt was not yet true, rebuked the Cross, and the bill for his wanton dishonour was still to be given. Markus turned his back and plunged face first into the desert. The grains entered his throat. Markus succumbed to the dust of his creation...

III : wounded spirit

Despite the soot and gaping holes, Markus could still 'see' what had once been the hall built by his father to commemorate the return of his prodigal son; he never saw that day. The Church may as well build a monument to the Betrayer and call it sacred; the hall had been converted to a public provision house the very day Markus had learned of its existence, three winters past.

A heaped black mass caught his eye. He turned to see wh—the pain shot through his rib cage, stopping in his lungs, forcing a cough that left behind the taste of blood mixed with acrid sourness.

"The physician said to remain in your bed for at least another half-fortnight," a strong feminine voice said from over Markus's shoulder; he did not turn around to meet his sister: Dawnlyn, Lady of Audaciter-Deus.

"You know where I rank the words of physicians."

"Even if that man be a true Hospitaller Knight?"

"The same Hospitaller that would see me in Jerusalem by season's end." Now Markus turned to meet his kin. She was tall in stature and wise in her councels, both given and accepted. Her leadership, with Markus in the Holy Land and their father's death, had kept the Norman bandits thwarted in their secret efforts to depose the Saxons of the surrounding land, had also been the steadying arm preventing certain Saxon Houses from plunging themselves headlong into a mortal fate. "How can I protect our family and its holdings if I am a world away?" Markus finished.

Dawnlyn flicked her eyes down. "It is seldom you are *not* a world away." She touched his arm with sisterly gentleness; her voice was hushed. "My dear Markus, nearly three autumns have passed since Jerusalem fell. I often perceive you alone in your quarters sitting for hours looking out your window to a world unseen, bustling with memory and conscience."

"And Holy God," added Markus.

Dawnlyn cocked her head slightly and released him from her touch sighing with shortness, and gently. "To hear you these last months, God has not been with you since you returned—as if you believe yourself the reason for the destruction of a whole army."

"I say this?"

"Your eyes and your actions scream this, Markus."

Markus let disgust creep into his voice. "And

what does my bearing say now if you can read your sibling like a seer?"

She turned away from him, offended by the remark. Markus accepted this. He could not determine where it was that Dawnlyn intended this conversation to go. This unsettled him: he hoped that affronting her would out the purpose, or discourage his sister from her course entirely.

"I am no seer, brother," she turned back to him with a visage normally reserved for politics, or suspicious Norman officials, "but it is a gift to a woman from God to be able to read that which men do not so freely give."

She had conquered the last of his defences. She would not be intimidated into a mistake, neither would she allow shallow words to upend her purpose. "You have never spoken this way to me before."

"I do not speak for myself alone."

They had come to it: her purpose was for two. The tone in her voice was like a mustering bell from beyond the horizon. All that was left was an appeal to the blood they shared. "If you love me, my sister, have caution on your next words."

Her face released none of its tension: whatever was to come next, it was from one appreciating the burden of a message difficult to deliver, difficult to receive. "You must lay yourself open to Mairín—your feelings, and your past." Markus tried to spin away, but Dawnlyn was quick to block the move with her hand upon his wrist. "She still holds a hope that the boy she loved will yet return to her. That he stands before her now, still unwilling to love, breaks her heart."

Markus did not know what to say. Once he had been unwilling, but now he was unable. Officially, he was still a member of the Templars and thus bound to their laws of celibacy. Some would perceive this an easy battlement to cower behind. Yet even if it did not exist there were other difficulties.

"Is it your intention to continue to silence your heart?"

She waited; Markus could feel there was more.

"She desires a child," his sister added; disappointment was rising in her voice. "Do you know this?"

"And I cannot break my oath to the Red Cross. Do *you* not know this?" Markus turned, with enough force that his sister could not prevent it this time. She was saying more on the subject but he did not hear her. How could he reply to this emotional siege without making the whole thing collapse upon him? "She cannot have the man she has chosen."

"She could. Sir Honour is dead to the Templar Order."

"But not to God."

"Holy God gave you to each other, Markus! But you hearkened to other voices."

Awkward silence seemed to expand to the birds and other creatures on the whole land. Markus noticed only the muted sound of the wind passing over the estate, as if trying to tiptoe past the contending descendents of Edelstan the Steadfast.

"You had a fever the first nights during your most recent recovery," Dawnlyn continued. "You cried out the name of Sir Honour, and for one named 'Percy', many times during these fits. Sir Charle and I covered as well as we could but Mairín knows there are tales untold."

Markus shook his head in anticipation of what he knew was coming next. "Do not ask this of me."

"It is too late; she is already waiting." She interrupted another plea: "Even if she is scarred by your words, you must tell her *everything*, Markus."

Dawnlyn held his gaze: she was right; he owed Mairín at least the dignity of not being left to endless wonder, to dream up heroics or nightmares with no confirmation of truth; hopelessly waiting for him, thus remaining alone without knowing the blessings of motherhood. But his sister needed to understand the potential implications of her order.

"If I tell her the things I must, then in the same hour I am surely doomed to Outremer." Markus was disheartened to observe his sister search the ground: she had reached a similar conclusion before his words, but there was more to communicate.

"Before he left, the Hospitaller identified the archer he disabled as the same man he saw riding on the road the day he arrived. We could not get him to speak coherently on the attack: he was Catalan; the other captives were either from the northern lands, or

Italians who spoke Vulgar Latin. Our spies returned little news as well. But it is confirmed that four other Saxon lords have all been attacked over the last two months by similar bands of men." She took a short, frustrated breath, looked at him with resolve. "These mercenaries, or more accurately their contractors, believe one of us to be harbouring a traitor, sought by Rome itself. If it is you they seek we will protect you."

She paused; his sister wanted to make sure that Markus understood the weight of the situation, and her loyalty to him.

She added, with great sympathy and concern: "What is it you have done to warrant such zealous attention?"

Markus was at a complete loss. The Templars rarely sought aid from Church authorities in legal matters; in their unique sovereignty they had no requirement to do so. If disciplinary action or fault was brought to the attention of the Order, they took care to apprehend the accused and hear the Knight's case before their own council. But could his sins have been judged so grievous as to set the whole world after his person? In an effort to remain open before God, only the abbot of Stevington had been confided in concerning his true name—left behind so as not to attract unnecessary Norman attention, either at home or afar. As far as the Templars were concerned the benefactor of 'Sir Honour' was the House of Audaciter-Deus—this so that the Curia would see what good use this Saxon House was to the Church. But the true country of one going by the name 'Honour' could not be easily detected by anyone suspicious or seeking trouble, as the word was akin in Frankish and Latin dialects; the word in the Saxon tongue (*weorþ*), rarely heard upon English roads since 'the Conqueror', bore no similarity.

Markus knew every person in the fiefdom—none were out of place; all were duly treated in Christian charity for its own sake and would see no value in a bribe.

Regardless, if his service with the Templars affirmed anything it was that man is a fickle beast: none are immune to the whisperings of the dark one. Markus and his sister could not know the minds of every person connected to their lordship in totality.

Dawnlyn moved a lock of hair out of his face. "We *love* you, Markus. If I thought this was only about politics I would never ask you to go back to the land that took your happiness. Even so, I feel in my heart this is a journey you must undertake, as much for yourself—and God—as for us."

Markus closed his eyes, and the world slowed to the pace of stars moving across the heavens.

IV : distant horizons

Mairín was waiting, but Markus did not invite her into his chamber. She was busy with weaving-craft beside a window in an alcove near the door. She did not look to him, did not make a single move that indicated she was aware of his entering his quarters.

But she knew. The dear woman would give him some time to sort his thoughts, although this would be a fruitless exercise. Instead he would use the minutes she granted him to begin a letter that would be left for her keeping.

He had barely written beyond the first lines of that note when a soft knock landed upon the door.

He sighed and replaced the quill pen: he could not compose the letter rightly until Audaciter-Deus was asleep. "Come." He gathered his pipe from the table, went about lighting it to calm his anxiety.

When he looked up: Mairín, clasping her hands loosely in front of her. She did her best to look composed for this defining point in her life. Even though her roots ran to the Germanic region of Thuringia, her stateliness came from her family's long association with the Roman-Saxon pedigree of Audaciter-Deus. Thus he could be frank with her.

He stood—found it impossible to even look at her. Retreating from his chair to his favourite window. He opened the top portion wide and thanked God for the clean fragrance of English twilight. In his view was the handsome chapel, built by his forefather, Markus II—receiver of this wonder-filled land from Offa, king of Mercia. He closed his eyes, inhaled once more (deeply), and forced out his unease. "The man you loved is dead, Mairín. I spoke of this end when I first left, eight Springs past."

"Life plays a cruel trick, forcing us to relive painful hours of youth." Her voice carried the pain of a scarred wound freshly injured, but it did not break.

Markus focused on two dancing gulls from the *Mare Nostrum*: one broke off, disappearing into the horizon like a spectre. "If there is cruelty in this meeting then it is of my own craft. Only the LORD God is able to design good and see it out."

He turned, indicating a chair nearby where Mairín stood. He remained standing so that he could linger in the crisp twilight air.

"You have come to know the name of one 'Sir Honour'," said Markus, confirming what she had heard him uttering during his fevers. He glossed over the reasons, keeping details such as confiding in the abbot at St. Mary's out of the telling. Markus told of some of his first experiences and the friends he had made amongst his brethren: spoke at greater length of his closest friend, Crispin; found it knotty to define Percy; reflected most fondly of Jacques de Mailly, his beloved captain and commander of the Templars in the Land of Jerusalem.

Markus came to Hattin, and breathed once before recounting for the first time in words what had, until now, been only torturous memory: "The battle was wrought from politics and petty rivalries. Despite my protestations, and those of a few others of my Knightly brethren, he was ordered to join the death march. On the eve of the encounter every bone and muscle rebelled: despite having occupied the best defensive ground, we were ordered forth. The Christian army went to be slaughtered, but Sir Honour remained behind—hidden among a collection of tall boulders, beneath a large overhang of rock." Markus searched for the best way to continue; his recollections of events after Hattin were somewhat sketchy. "After a time Sir Honour came to learn the Most Holy Cross of Our LORD was captured by the Muslims and vilely desecrated. Protecting the Holy Cross was his—was *my* charge, Mairín."

She pondered his story. Markus watched the hearth-glow ford the weaving rush of gold to the gentle slopes of her face, finding the ridge not high but still impassable, thus flanking round to the plain of her brow, barely achieving the crest of her crown.

"God does not condemn fear or shame brought on by the foolishness of men."

"Would that I was merely shamed by men for running from a battle! I care little for the verdicts of ignorant men. My shame comes in the shadow of Holy God." Markus regretted that she would now discover certain truths in a manner she did not deserve. "I did not turn from battle because I feared death. I turned from battle because I feared I would never set my eyes upon *you* again! In the years following my departure, I found my love for you, Maírín. I was afraid I would die before..." Further words died because he did not have the vocabulary. The Holy Orders did not train a man in the way of love. There was only time to regain strength in the body, perform the Mass at the appointed times, reflect on how to maintain faithfulness in one's commitment made to Christ—specifically for him: to guard the Church, within the framework of preserving the outlier kingdom and keeping safe the roads of penance and commerce.

The great happiness that rose in her eyes lanced across his heart. She did not understand. "By not taking up my charge for Christ, and protecting His Cross and those bearing it, I placed *you* before *Him*: that is a grievous act, be he a knight or a common man."

Now the joy became sorrow—but not that of a burden shared. "You lay the consequences of your decision to take up a banner of Christendom at my feet as well as your own? As if I caused you to seek the service of arms in a foreign land? Recall that I knew your father as well, and his spoken desire that you stay here, with your family. Your choice was solely yours, Markus, and none could talk you away from your course in those final days among us. You knew well the feelings of all those who loved you, or you would not have left under cover of night and when your Father and Mother were on business away from this land. How dare you lay blame and burden on those undeserving!"

Markus sat down, stunned at the rightness that assaulted his conscience.

Mairín kneeled at his feet and placed a hand on his cheek. All evidence of her rebuke was faded. "Surely, for the sake of Christ, God will forgive you, Markus. We are creatures prone to weakness. Divine Providence brought you out of those trials. Do you not see His love for us all in this?"

Markus's head was on a swivel; ache entered his throat; his gaze was far away: "I could not be prone to the weakness you speak. Right or wrong, I took an *oath*, Mairín—an oath to God to serve Him without limit or diversion. My failure allowed the highest form of desecration to His Tool of Pinnacle Sacrifice, from which all have been redeemed. He has never abandoned me, this House. But I—" Markus swallowed. "No, God will not forgive this egregious sin; not yet. Not until I return to Outremer and face the due punishment."

He looked into Mairín's darkening eyes. Markus could tell his words were at war with her understanding. She loved him dearly and did not know how to reconcile his authority and attitude with what her spirit was telling her. He was causing anguish in her presence, and he feared that he clinging to his despondent nature might corrupt her faith. Indeed, it was better for him to be cut off from his family than to steer them onto the same wide course to perdition. "Milady: I *must* be like a ghost to you."

She withdrew her hand. Tears did not come; it was an effort of unyielding trust tempered by fervent prayer.

Her resoluteness humbled the Lord of Audaciter-Deus; he told her so. She had breached all defences; he was overrun; he did not tell her this, for she would not find him in the smoking ruin wrought by her faith and love.

"I mourned the death of my dreams long ago," she responded, her voice on the brink of crashing. Defiance against another reality set her delicate brow, bending the tips: nothing of this last hour would have passed between them if the question of his leaving was not perceived to be tipping against them.

Markus was turned from her now, gazing at some invisible thing through the window; the ambient landscape was descending violet as the twilight came upon them rapidly. "Place the pain of your conscience in me. Let me carry your burden so that it may be swallowed by the Sacred Body of Christ."

Markus wondered if this unrelenting charity had been offered by God to make him a villein. "Only our LORD can ease this burden, milady. It will be in a trial of His choosing." *And I do not think he will end my guilt in the arms of the woman, whom was my only thought when the Sacred Cross needed my sword in its defence; though, truly, O LORD, the fault was none but mine own.*

Mairín's weakening eyes could bear the sight of the Saxon prince no longer.

Markus prayed this torture would not continue.

"I am sorry for you," she said finally, in a tone that was either genuine or severe disapproval.

Markus desperately wanted to ease the hurt. "Tell me to stay and I will consider this heavily against my road—even at the risk of the ire of God."

She turned back, her gaze full of resentment at his patronization. "Truly you were not so willing to consider this when your heart was filled with fear of being loved rather than divine wrath. So why should you consider it now, when your whole body shakes at the invocation of His Holy Name at Mass and good-natured conversation?"

So, he had not been merely called upon the penance road to Jerusalem, but indeed was already upon it: Each reproach and kindness from Mairín was surely God humbling him, preparing him for the *anfechtungen* that were to come; they could not be more painful—only more numerous.

"Have you resolved what the men sought in their attack upon us? Perhaps *there* is a task that God would allow, for the sake of your House and to consider the necessity of your leave-taking."

Markus's shoulders sagged at the eternal hope of this Godly creature. He sought sanctuary in the transcendent landscape outside the window, now fully mantled in night with its bright crown jewel refusing the darkness full reign. "Your words confirm my road, and why I cannot tarry." He turned with effort from the window scene. "The men who attacked this castle were paid swords, from lands varied. They were trained well, and not just to fight. There is little they can tell us we can trust. But they can be stopped if I am not here."

Her eyes wondered: *Hired by whom?*

"Only the Creator knows the hand that sent them, and He has used this band to press me on."

"Why so much dread towards a journey if you are but a pilgrim?"

Markus laughed; he regretted its mocking tone, for how could Mairín know the full reality in the Land of Christ. "My dear: should a Christian, by the will of God, survive the treacherous seas of water and sand, he cannot simply strut into Jerusalem, even for the sole purpose of his faith. At present the Saracen controls its sacred walls. Only a Christian who is expired or able to pay the tax is given leave to pass through Blessed Tancred's Gate; safety is not assured. Further: Percy was less than clear as to what awaits me in that Sacred Church of Our LORD's Tomb, which was reduced to ruin when Muslims last seized Jerusalem." For the first time the steep task was truly laid out before him. "Am I to brave all these things on a whim for a trinket or scroll bearing the wisdom of a dead man? I go as a shadow chasing the wind..."

"If God has called you there, then He will preserve you and provide a way to enter. For He delights in seeing His servants put the saving of a soul—especially their own—before all possession and doubt."

The calm strength in her voice, and the words that flowed with it, comforted him, and he felt a hope reach out its hand: *Oh that God would give me a new chance, but the guilt from my actions, found wanting in the Holy Scales, are strapped to this body.*

"Excepting my time with Sir Jacques, I have received more of Christ in your words than ever," Markus commented. And yet this given comfort seemed like water through parted fingers. He turned his focus to the sky: stars now appeared on the horizon, and one in particular seemed to dance on the far hill. Mairín's arm enclosed his waist; Markus had not the strength to refuse her this contact.

"Linger in your thoughts no longer, milord Markus. Keep a vigil in the chapel this night; receive the Mass at the dawn. If you have discerned in those hours by the grace of Holy God that it is right for you to achieve the end to which you have been called: then go to the Holy Sepulchre of our Lord Jesus in haste, so you may return to us that much sooner. For we value your life, but hold more dear your heart. If tribulation comes to these hills you may lose both if it is still so burdened."

A trinity of Christian voices with 'Outremer' from their lips to my ears: the LORD *God has truly called me.* Markus became overwhelmed with sorrow, yet turned to face the woman behind him. For the first time he looked up her countenance fully: a still water reflecting his foolishness. More appropriately than many a woman of proper pedigree did she deserve the title of one speaking at court. The next words choked him, like a condemned man forced to read his own fatal decree before the execution of the sentence. "Watch me close as I disappear over yonder horizon, Lady Mairín. I feel that sight will be the last this majestic land shall have of this cursed head."

Unable to abide the utter despair looking back at her, Mairín embraced Markus. She fought the tears with a broken shield beneath tattered banners—she would not give that ancient foe an opportunity to extinguish her hope. "If that be so then I shall look for you on a brighter horizon, my prince, and shall thereafter pray in fervor that Holy God would speed me to it."

V : into brittany

It was impossible for Lord of Audaciter-Deus to know his standing amongst the brothers of the Red Cross. Markus recalled the concealed Templar paths through the mainland of western Christendom, but they presently offered as much danger as any of the public roads he might take; he rarely set foot out of the shire, and never England, since his return. The name he had taken to hide his Saxon nobility, was just as much in exile as his person; Hattin, ironically, no longer made that name honourable to bear. So Markus had to remain content letting that life disappear somewhere between Heaven and Ibelin. He also did not want to be overlong in the kingdom where the Order was formed and held its greatest influence. This was the reason he chose to go east through minimal French country to the Teutonic realm of the *Imperium Romanum Sacrum*, then south to the sea. But this course meant the gravest risk: Champagne. And so the question presently deliberated in the waning sunlight was whether to travel as Markus or 'Sir Honour' when he reached the realm of Champagne—the birthplace and centre of the Templar world.

But first there was Brittany, which was no unified English country; that the Bretons maintained ill relations with the Normans for well past a century guaranteed nothing to a Saxon prince: his people had sided with the Normans against the Breton ruler, Conan II; not a year later certain Bretons had been counted with Duke William at Hastings. Henry II— still king of England despite his widely suspected ill health from age—kept the territory as a barn of dry hay near glowing cinders, using the divided villages to gain control. The simmering unrest against his rule persisted. A Templar however would likely pass through the English provinces unhindered by the machinations of royal courts (and Markus could risk the folk being ignorant of his unbearded face—a standard mark of Knight of the Temple).

His prayer was that the Bretons would accept him as a Saxon pilgrim traversing their lands, more likely an ally against their mutual Norman rival.

The mystery assaults upon Saxon houses continued to bother him. He considered other opponents outside the papal court. It was not outside the realm of possibility that the attackers, bearing no crest of country or house, could have been soldiers hired by the Norman overlords to please the Holy See by taking on tasks such as running down a fugitive—that he was Saxon made a ripe target. Prince John was despiteful, and anxiously ill-tempered, and sorely lacking in Godly fear: it was his pleasure to maltreat the former rulers; he desired to subvert the country to the extent that only 'Norman' would be seen and learned—as if the Saxon age should be considered nothing more than an accidental smudge on the chronicles. Richard would not approve (indeed the royal House was hardly ever in the country to disapprove), alone because the Saxon lords were now so few. So perhaps his motivation lay in a penance for his frequent transgressions that might pay a dividend in some future consideration where papal approval was needed?

The problem in charging the prince with retaining scoundrels was that his heir-apparent brother had emptied the coffers to fund his pilgrimage to release Jerusalem from the grip of Saladin. It was doubtful John had enough personal wealth to employ such vermin; certainly no skill of charm or intimidation.

Therefore, only one body possessed the resources necessary for such an anonymous campaign, outside the *Curia*: his own Order. He never had been able to shake the feeling they knew 'Sir Honour' was alive. It made sense: his superiors wanted answers, and satisfaction for his broken vow of "service to the last man".

After all, the Order of the Temple held many secrets; not quite those of the increasingly wild folk-lore that was tolerated for the intoxicating (if not intimidating) aura of powerful mystique, but the unique secrets of wealth management, which yielded the boon of leverage in politics—at least these were the secrets to which 'Sir Honour' had been directly privy. Markus had sometimes caught whispers of affairs more enigmatic: advanced knowledge learned from distant civilizations concerning all manners of subjects from architecture to machines to undiscovered lands beyond the known seas.

Then, for the first time in many seasons, Markus recalled that his captain and teacher, Sir Jacques de Mailly, had bequeathed to him an offspring of one of these advancements: a book, which immediately demonstrated its immense value when Markus had seen its pages.

The slow plodding of his horse threatened to put him to sleep and his mind wandered back to his original thoughts: What else might the Order hold, down deep? The tales of the Order, recounted by common folk over rounds of brew after another laborious day, were certainly intended to enliven the monotony of their lives. Yet every story begins with something true, or is designed to deceive truth; de Mailly had been careful to instruct his knights that survival included never *pouf*-ing off an accounting received of events, no matter how remarkable: all parts had to be pondered and deliberated, also the source—indeed the greatest truths of the faith had been hidden beneath the layers of parables by the LORD Jesus Christ Himself. And what of the miracles He performed while walking the roads of Judea, and those of His Passion, and after His Ascension—

miracles so numerous that not all were detailed, or even recorded, in the Holy Writ? More so: Christ was alive—the God of the Testaments Who had done so many wonder-full things for His people whether Incarnate, Unseen, or Spirit. Therefore His Church had to be vigilant, lest a great sign of His Hand visit her children and they be found asleep. And yet: chapels, cathedrals, monasteries, abbeys, knightly Orders, noble Houses, realms, and towns all strived to be seen as the most holy, the most pious, the most blessed—temporal gain never seemed very far from the signs and relics encouraged from pulpits to country roads.

Would such an immense gift as a True Sign or a Divine Artefact be given from Heaven in this age— even for the endurance of the *Ecclesia Militans*—while Christendom struggled so mightily in the snare of eminence?

An unnatural movement of several low branches in the windless afternoon returned his immediate attention to his present surroundings. Markus placed a hand on the cross-inlaid pommel of Audacit'in-Domino and studied his the surroundings. He heard no strange 'signal callings', saw no further movements.

"What is your business on this road?"

Markus swallowed his racing heart back to its place, thinking how best to answer the handsome Norman voice that spoke out of sight from behind; it was likely supported by a ready sword, and companions.

"Speak quickly, Saxon," came the steady command.

Markus needed time. "How do you know I am—"

"We have watched you since you came upon these shores."

"I am in the land of the King of England."

"These are not the King's roads. How did you come upon them?"

"I do not think you would believe me, sir."

"What is your name?"

Markus was not confident either answer would satisfy the man. Unless he changed the situation at hand, all further questions would be pressed by a Templar council—for the voice certainly belonged to one of Markus's Knightly kin.

Markus kicked his mount into action and enjoyed a decent head-start on whoever would be pursuing him. A quick glance over his shoulder confirmed two horsemen not a hundred feet behind; another quick glance promised he would be in their captivity soon if he did not attempt to be a more challenging target.

He veered off the road, his steed bounding over a shrub into a small forest. He set his feet firmly in the stirrups, prepared to make a sharp turn to the right as soon as he cleared the tree-line.

He was out of the forest and into the brilliant sunlight; something about the intensity made Markus think of what it might have been like for the disciples to witness the transfiguration of Christ—

His horse reared up and nearly over: Markus found himself rushing to the ground. The impact whipped his head into the winter-hardened earth; washed colour burst in his eyes; he felt footfalls approaching; a voice said something, as if yelling over flatland from half a league away. The world tilted out of view, into the darkness.

VI : Sir Honour and the Templars

The distant gurgling of water greeted Markus's confused ears. His eyes opened slowly: orange light splashed the grey stone walls; hazy shapes formed into a long table with three white-cloaked men seated behind; others—totalling eleven—stood in no less than pairs in corners, guarding doors, flanking the table.

The *gurgling* was not water, but the sound of hushed voices. And when the figures, draped in various kits of role and rank of the Knights of the Temple of Solomon, saw their captive was awake and now sitting on the cot all sound ceased as if cut off by a knife.

"You have caused us considerable trouble, Sir Honour." It was the centre man at the table who spoke in such a measured voice; his drawn accent (and carefully articulated) was a curious blend of Christendom: truly, the man had seen posts in many countries, taken in the culture and language, and therefore was unlikely to be disposed to any one as a favourite.

"I suppose he has," Markus bluffed; the gathering had yet to provide evidence they were convinced he was the man they thought he was.

Markus focused on the inquisitor: a lightly tanned and taut face that had weathered at least two score of life, the receding hair coloured grey and dulled-sand, pulled into a long tail that fell over one shoulder; the dual-toned scarlet cape of exceptional Damascus cloth, which his waking eyes had falsely perceived as mere reflection from the torches, marked him as one in charge of the highest affairs; the more ornate 'Cross fleury' upon the shoulder stood out from its inch-thick silver border indicating the considerable rank of Land-Marshal (all other Templars—knights and ranking officers—bore a simple version of the 'Cross pattée' or the 'Cross moline'). There were never more than two of this rank in the Order: one for Christendom, one for Outremer; the rank sat just below the Grand Master and his Seneschal. The sight of the Red Fleury kindled memory of his beloved captain, who had (too briefly) achieved Land-Marshal of the Latin states-east.

"If you are not the Templar named," the Marshal responded carefully, "how did you come by the tunic and ring of this Order that was found in your possession; such a Knight is not relieved of these items with ease."

"I do apologize for being upon your road, good sirs. My lord and I were separated in the night by a party of Norman bandits. He gave me the items you discovered so as to protect his identity—of utmost value to his purpose. My lord was heading for the Sicilian coast and I hoped to meet with him there." His stomach fell; Markus remembered the words of the Knight who had stopped him on the road: *We have watched you since you came upon these shores*—which meant they would have noticed he had been travelling alone, unless they had not been committed to observing him. Markus paused, trying to read if any of the men were buying the tale. But reading the face of a collection of veteran Templars was like reading the face of God Himself. *God*—He was the key to getting out of this! "Perhaps our Almighty Creator deigned me upon this road to be your ally in the search for the knight you seek. I am happy to relay any message you may have for him."

The council looked at each other in turn, then leaned and discussed in hushed words, movements of the head, gestures with thumbs and fingers. Finally they resumed their official posture and the Marshal spoke: "You can tell your master simply that he is in grave danger. He is to report to this council in all possible haste. You are free to go with this urgent message."

Markus got up from the crude bed and took tentative steps towards the thick wooden door from which two guards stepped aside. He replayed the words in his head; certain syllables held genuine concern in their cadences. They were desperate to find

Sir Honour and could not take the chance to detain Markus when he exhibited no clear danger to them. But it was also probable that he would be followed, and with more closeness. And there was this: Was it possible their distress was connected to those who had attacked his House, in the sense his Order knew the identities and sought to aid a Christian estate?

Markus was at an impasse. These men were of his cloth. Sure there were foul men in the ranks, but these were often brash, claiming their "Christian" tithes and supplications and success against merchant raids as evidence of their "great faith" and God's acknowledgement of the same when their success and "piety" enriched their personal coffers. But these men of the council—or at least the Marshal who spoke—were as noble in their sin-tainted flesh as any Christian Markus called 'friend' or 'brother'.

Markus remained facing away from his brothers. "How did you know I did not perish?" He heard quickening footsteps. He turned his head: the Marshal was already nearly upon him.

"God be praised He has led you to us!"

Curiosity wrinkled Markus's brow. "Then my capture is not sought by the Order?"

"Your....*person* was sought by this council," the Marshal said, selecting the emphasised word with delicacy "after reports reached us of the facts of Hattin."

Markus shook his head, still convinced that all was a trap to get him to admit some hidden truth.

"Then the raids upon my kin in my homeland are not by command of the Order?"

The Marshal moved his arm back to his side; his eyes became slits for a moment. "This is new to me, Sir Honour" he said. Markus believed him (there was no reason to correct his usage of 'Sir Honour'; it might be useful to keep 'Markus' disconnected from the Order). "We would not ravage a country to capture one of our own; I think you know that we are well-informed to need such crass means to an end. So it seems another seeks you also, and dangerous if he defies a papal edict."

Markus watched the Marshal return to the table and gather up his parchments. Then he turned to a nearby door and opened it. The Templar officer paused before crossing the threshold and looked to Markus: "Walk with me."

In the flickering light of the fortress corridor, Markus studied the man to his left with occasional glances.

"You are wondering if you can trust me," he said finally after the long silence. The Marshal had stopped by a flanking set of doors, and then exhaled solemnly. "What a world we are building when a brother in Christ is not sure he can trust a fellow brother." Now he turned to look at Markus. "Faith needs to extend as much to your fellow man, Sir Honour, as it must extend to God."

"Faith in men?" inquired Markus. Something did not ring true.

"Faith in man's desire to be good and true..." the Marshal rapped upon the doors, which opened "...just as our Creator is good and true. Did Sir Jacques never speak of this to you?" Beyond the doors a servant was completing a table laden with food and drink. Markus turned back to the Marshal, who now wore an hospitable smile reflecting his manner. "Let us eat," he added, "and talk."

The day was waning, but urgency did not. Following a turn off the same corridor from the room where they had feasted, the Land-marshal brought Markus to a room that could hold one hundred twenty-five brother-Knights comfortably. The maps on tables and one stretched between two columns, the strategy tools, the four armour models, and an array of displayed weaponry organised upon racks and tables were clear in their purpose: the Order was planning a significant campaign in Outremer.

"What would you say to being Commander of Knights, to aid in the retaking of Jerusalem?"

Markus looked to the Marshal and realised that the man had been watching him. So he approached a window and allowed a measure of time to pass to give the Marshal the impression he was weighing the offer. In truth he was confused: What good had he done to be worthy of such a title? Perhaps it was a test of his integrity.

"I would say, 'With respect: I decline.'"

Markus turned and found the Marshal not

looking surprised at his response. The lingering silence meant the Templar *Parat in Europa* still wanted his reasons.

"To retake Jerusalem will require tens of thousands of noble men; such an army must be committed to the preservation of the city and protecting the weak if it hopes to have the favour of Heaven. Just as important: enough of those noble men would need to survive the years of march, temptation, and battle to arrive at the City, and then—should the final assault yield success by the grace of God— defend her against the sure attacks to follow."

Markus expected the Marshal would quickly rescind his good nature towards him with the words that were about to follow. He stepped closer and leaned on the nearest table to drive home his primary reason. "And Outremer has enough hawkish officers and fickle princes."

The Knight considered his superior before finishing, who remained stoic: either the man was skilled at hiding emotion until the proper time in discourse, or he knew the words Markus spoke were true. The reality of the man's nature would soon be revealed as Markus had arrived at the harshest of his criticisms. "I would not trust my person with a rank in this order, milord. For I would see removed from all authority the likes of Gerard de Ridefort and the puppet-king, Guy de Lusignan, before I would turn to the armies of the caliphates."

Now the Marshal bristled. "These names rank

high in Christendom, sir—including the former, who is *this Order's* Master. Why do you seek to burn them with the fire in your eyes?"

Markus should have been in irons at the treason he had spoken, not further entertained. Before Hattin, he had never been vocal in his opposition to these men during his service; it was taught that the battlefield was where the focus needed to remain. The opinions he provided the councils from time to time were always refined in deep discussion with men like Percy, and his captain.

Again, Markus recalled, he held no rank in the Order, nor had he performed any remarkable action of valour that would give someone such as a prestigious Land-Marshal any reason to honour his words as an equal. Either he was being tested for a purpose to be revealed, or his brothers wanted Markus to build his own gallows. He gave his senior officer a look that communicated he would not continue until the man had spoken.

"You had more to say at Sephoria," the officer prodded.

So the Order was aware of his censures. It made sense that his requested audience before King Guy had been duly recorded, and had reached the eyes of the *couvent*. Markus had not been the only critic of Guy's plan to march on Saladin, but the opposition included persons that Ridefort personally despised, thus motivating him to harden Guy's resolve to break camp from what was otherwise an advantageous position for the Christian army.

The Marshal was surely tolerating his lacking discretion for a clear purpose. No other reason made sense.

Except perhaps one other: Was God providing him a favourable season to influence a new direction—at the least, to serve Christendom and die with some honour restored? If so, then it was his obligation to make full use of the platform—even if it meant his death.

"Guy is a spineless, foppish devil-spawn, and Ridefort—" Markus turned aside his head sharply to hide the rush of loathing that trembled his lips and put a sting in his eyes. "You have heard of Cresson," he managed, "just months before Hattin?"

"Of course: an accursed massacre, which saw the death of a promising Land-Marshal of Outremer in Sir Jacques; also the Blessed Master of our Hospitaller brethren, Roger de Moulins. There were but a few nameless survivors, including Master Ridefort. What is your authority on the matter?"

"The authority of *experience*, lord Marshal." Markus locked his gaze on his superior and stood, baring his chest: a long scar winded from the left pectoral down to his torso. "Ridefort blamed Saint George for abandoning us." Markus continued through the sneer of his lip. "I blame our 'blessed' Master for abandoning his created senses and reason—*seven thousand Saracens*, and barely a hundred fifty in our number."

The Templar officer's eyes widened, and he spoke as one who had just been grossly offended by a slap to his face. "The account we received had your defending ranks at least half their number?!"

"Defending?!" Markus spat the word out like a mouthful of poisonous berries. "We were the *attacking* force, milord, victimised by the worst kind of evil."

"Details, man. Details!"

Markus could not tell if the Marshal was angry at him, or at those who allegedly had falsified vital records. He explained how much Ridefort enjoyed the rivalry of the Templar and Hospitaller orders; how Jacques and Roger, loved by their commands, had little for Outremer's supreme military commander or his puppet-king. Then Markus uncovered memories he preferred remain buried in the deep:

"Ridefort mocked Sir Roger and Sir Jacques, answering their protestations with suggestions of cowardice and apostasy if they did not follow him in a charge upon the Muslims in the valley. Certainly both knew they would die in such a reckless act of war, but they took comfort for Christendom that Ridefort would surely join them in that end. Led by the Templar and Hospitaller banners, we charged the Muslim force."

Markus continued by detailing how Jacques and Roger fought as the greatest warrior-saints, despite the inevitable defeat; he noted that Ridefort remained on the outskirts of the battle. And when all Christian attackers were perceived to be destroyed,

Ridefort fled. "I witnessed this vile treachery, but could do nothing as I lay wounded beneath a heap of slain and dying. By sheer rage did I manage myself free, and by the mercy of God did Balian de Ibelin overtake me before my succumbing to the trial."

The Marshal swallowed, not able to look Markus in the face. "Will you swear to this account before Holy God?"

"I will. I gave the master of Ibelin this same account while in his hospice, though I do not know his fate after Jerusalem fell."

"I appreciate this may not comfort you, Sir Honour, but the deaths of your brethren at Cresson caused Prince Raymond to repent of his dalliance with Saladin," the Templar officer pointed out.

"And if Raymond had not been the aim of treachery overseen by Ridefort, then all events are null." The Master did not abide rivals or opposition; 'the faith' was a means to the ends he planned for himself; he considered it brilliant wisdom to destroy challengers rather than to contend with them: Jacques and Roger would have found their deaths by his design, at some other dark hour if not Cresson.

The Marshal thought on this, pacing just two full trips then saying: "How can you conclude all of this so boldly?"

"Does not the stall smell fouler to the one cleaning the barn, than to those labouring in the house? I seek no glory or reward with my words. What have I to lose that the Order and Holy God do not already possess?"

Markus dared to step closer to the Marshal; he felt that he had a momentary advantage to plead for a view that he had long held from his experiences as a Knight in the Land of Christ. If he did not press now, even briefly, he may never get a second opportunity. Further, he felt the urge to prove to the officer that he was not an enemy.

"Milord, why is the perception allowed that communion with God is stronger in one city or country over any other? Control of Jerusalem does not water the seeds of faith—coveting and murder are the primary fruits harvested there."

The Marshal pressed a finger upon his mouth and looked up at Markus for a long uncomfortable minute. "I begin to see why you felt it necessary to 'die' before setting foot again on these shores. Your words have many implications, none which would please papal wolf-callers."

The hair on Markus's arms stood on end, and he retreated a few unsteady steps. Had he erred in trusting this man too much? Had he simply crossed the line, and now a potential ally could no longer protect him?

The Templar senior officer placed both hands on the pommel of his sword. "Many Knights of rank agree with your words. But Rome cannot be batted away like a horsefly. Jerusalem must be taken and the True Cross reclaimed: in these endeavours the Templar banner must be among the boldest." He lifted a defiant chin to accentuate those words, and those that were about to follow. "You swore an oath to the Order by Holy God, Sir Honour. Do you intend to break that vow?"

Markus raised his own head. "Not so long as the Red Cross serves Heaven and His Incarnate Word above all."

"You doubt the integrity of your Brothers?"

"With Ridefort as Master, and Guy as an ally of the Red Cross...?"

"What if I could restore your faith in the Order... prove to you that these men are only so much smoke?"

Markus suppressed a sigh. "Too much smoke leads to a cry of 'fire', milord. If the Order desires God's favour, why allow such men to be our face?"

The Marshal put out his hands, one that indicated the door. "Let me show you, sir Knight. Let me reveal things to which few are privy."

"I have spoken words that should see a man stripped of all station, if not brought to the justice of the noose."

"I have faith in you." The Marshal reached into his cloak and brought out a roll of parchment. "Because Sir Jacques had faith..."

He extended the parchment to Markus, which he took. His eyes skimmed the Latin even as he unrolled it. He was out of practice with the tongue and could not perceive much. But he recognised his name, certain phrases that his captain indeed used, the sign from his hand at the end.

Markus rolled up the scroll, handing it back to the Marshal and pressing against the aching in his eyes with his thumb and finger. "I need not your evidence, lord Marshal, and I declare again my unworthiness: have no faith in my wayward desire to be true. Let me pass on my way with your blessing; you have my promise of silence."

The scroll was tucked away; both the Marshal's hands settled upon his sword pommel once more. "Silence is for cowards."

"Was not Christ silent before His enemies?"

"We are not your enemies, Sir Honour, nor Christendom's! We serve God in the best way sinful men can; do not confuse our lack of admonition with affirmation, or complicity. Guy and Gerard make their war so the Order can prepare for its own. The atrocities they commit will be judged by Holy God in His time."

"And also ours, for turning a blind eye to innocents murdered without mercy or charity, even as the Name of Christ pours from our mouths. You cannot justify forbearance of such God-less leaders with the delusion that ends unseen will benefit the Kingdom of God. Heaven will not abide such brazen hypocrisy—it has not!"

The Marshal's scowl implied his patience was close to spent. "Very well. Kill Guy. Kill Gerard. Will that rid us from the Saracens, or the spiritual rot which you condemn so righteously? Who else will take their place? Might they commit far worse deeds?"

Markus thought of Jacques: he always had the right words. Wait! His captain had *given* him the words. "We must defend our neighbours against a people that would have their enemies bow the knee to their religion at the tips of swords. Our rulers are right to command us destroy an army that preys upon simple pilgrims harming none in their humble piety. I will be first to lead a charge against such adversaries. Yet I have perceived deeper ambitions lurking beneath these good works: We crave a peace of banners waving in every parapet on earth; a foolish task, for we cannot bear the sight of any banner but that of our own country. Our LORD says His is the Peace, like none other, for which we must strive—indeed the Pure Light of His Peace overpowered the pitch darkness of the very Empire that placed Him on a wretched cross and persecuted His saints. Christendom is so anxious over every step of the Muslim, distracting us all from brotherhood, even while Christ assures us He has overcome the world. Do we forget David, Moses and Joshua, Abraham? For the sake of His glory, and the love of His people, did God deliver every foe into their hand."

"No, Sir Honour, our Order has not forgotten." A look of interest softened the Marshal's defensive posture. "Your words are well-spoken. You have learned them from another."

The first real feeling of panic began to wax in Markus's chest. After his training, Markus had been assigned to Acre under the command of Jacques de Mailly. Markus—all the men under his command—loved the captain. Before the Mass he sometimes taught them from a hand-sized book, otherwise carried near his chest. Just before the charge at Cresson, Jacques had pulled Markus aside and wordlessly handed him the book. As his captain had done, he kept the book securely inside his tunic, believing Jacques had wanted him to return it to the Order.

During his extended hospice in Jerusalem after Cresson, Markus came to befriend his Hospitaller caretaker, Sir Percy. He eagerly inquired about the book as soon as Markus was strong enough to talk (as it had been discovered on his person by Percy). Not realizing what he possessed, Markus declined. The Knight persisted; Markus opened the book and realised why Jacques had been able to speak and teach with such remarkable authority.

The book was marked as being the Gospel of Saint John the Evangelist; it was in the *Norman* tongue, not the Latin of the *Vulgate*. The majority of Christendom outside the cloister could not read, and it was not encouraged; the Writ was presented as a "dark book" susceptible to the rashness of man, as a great burden upon minds—indeed, recalling Moses' grim warning of what would happen to a man or beast who even touched the Holy Mountain of God, were all believers admonished (even the ordained) as to the risk of Divine retribution from delving unprepared into the Holy Message. Further, never had Markus heard of a copy of the Word translated for a tongue besides *ecclesia* Latin or Greek. It had been easy for Markus to feign ignorance on the provenance of the book. Engrossed with its contents, Percy seemed to care little for its origins; Markus agreed to lend it to him for a few days.

Then the orders had come to meet Saladin at Tiberius, with Markus joining the Templars that would guard the Holy Cross. He had never seen Percy again, nor the priceless translation of the gospel. He was sure Percy had been with the Christian host. But in his haste to flee on the eve of Hattin, all thoughts of things such as scandalous books and sacred vows were strangely far from his mind; the air of fear and guilt and love-sickness had been smothering.

The eyes of the senior Knight appeared to be watching the scene of a vision far away. With a blink he was focused on Markus again; a glint in his pupils not only remained, it had increased. "Jacques was one of those chosen by the *couvent* because of his great desire to see our Order succeed." The Marshal clasped Markus's forearm. "He thought much of you, Sir Honour, or he never would have entrusted you with the book."

The compliment quickened Markus's heart. But on its heels was the reminder of his abandonment of his duties, the abandonment of Mairín; the warmth quickly cooled as a hearth with a waning flame. Thus he made no acknowledgment.

"I am convinced," the Marshal continued with

rising assurance, "to open up to you the unseen world of the Red Cross. At the end you may choose how to approach the next stage of your journey."

Markus lowered his head; raising it again, he gripped the wrist of the Marshal (still grasping his forearm) with approving strength. "I accept this invitation, milord."

Happiness broke across the officer's face. "I am glad!" —and he struck the shoulder of Markus with firm approval.

VII : the path to honour

The tunnels twisted and the turns were sudden: they remained in the tight torch-lit passage for such a length of time that Markus expected to emerge in another country. His Templar brothers appeared to be playing a perilous game. Even in exile word had reached his ears that much of Christendom bound the loss of Jerusalem and the Holy Cross firmly upon the shoulder of the Red Cross. And why not? The Templars possessed rare autonomy as a holy Order, were known to have the best training, had the most success in battle, earned the most fear; Saladin showed mercy to every type of Christian, but for Templars and Hospitallers the fate was always the same: death. The Red Cross had amends to make, and wrongs to correct. If the Curia discovered the Order were not wholly eyes-on-target regarding the re-acquisition of Jerusalem, Markus wondered if the Holy See would dare turn all of Christendom against them. The Templars' increasing wealth of resources and vast influence were more than enough reason.

Thus as the public front of the Order, Master Gerard de Ridefort, and his very real ambition and bloodlust would convince interested eyes the Templars were committed to Outremer.

Markus recalled one particular night gathering with Jacques and his brothers, in a damp cavern, nearby the Mount of Olives; it was well into the season of *Quadragesima*. The men in his command had grown over-weary of the intense divisions at court of which their own Master was a chief machinator (and in no small part to blame for Raymond of Tripoli's treasonous act of a treaty with Saladin), of the promise of a vicious new war by Pentecost with the Sultan of Egypt when the current truce was ended (and who had spent months strengthening his Muslim force in Syria), of the exploitation of those entering the kingdom upon the pilgrim road by way of rival Italian access points leaving them the poorer and vulnerable to bandits (not four days earlier they had been deployed late—too late to help a group of such Christians, just two leagues from the Temple barracks, seeking shelter at Ein Karem).

Sir Jacques had looked upon his despondent brothers and said something near to what Markus now recalled:

Our LORD Jesus Christ spoke of His Kingdom being not from this terrestrial ball; the advent of His justice is still to come, when the passing of this world is placed at His righteous Hand. Through the Blessed Mass we abide in Him and He in us: we shall not be discouraged when cities and countries fall to unbelievers and ill-governance; Jerusalem,

Acre, Tyre, Antioch—even Rome itself—could descend into hell-fire, and still the Truest Kingdom would live on.

When death approaches hasten to the Light of Men with sword for our enemies and delight in your hearts! For what do we fight in this Blessed Land? As humble knights pledged to the LORD, we fight for our neighbours—be they spiritual kin or innocent neighbour! We fight for this more fiercely than any land or stone or banner: we serve in this place for that end alone; we submit to kings, regents, and masters because it is Holy God Who has given them authority to command us. Yet He has reserved the greater unseen realm as His sovereign domain, ruled by the Sacred Cross of His Passion.

When we fail, it is because we have acted as blind villains and must repent; this becomes the glory of God. This is our confession: Non nobis, non nobis, Domine, sed nomini tuo da gloriam.

The words of his captain brought forth such a welling of joy deep inside Markus's breast—the same he and his fellow Knights had felt in that hour, which endured and was nourished with more such words.

Love and unreleased grief buckled Markus's knees and blurred the hewn passage; he caught himself against the rock; the air was suddenly very close and breaths refused to fill his lungs. Now only Mairín's face was among his thoughts—dim, but there, as a face in poorly lit water. When he focused on her there was nothing but a reflection of the dark clouds upon the expanse of his mind.

The Marshal, unaware of the condition of his companion had continued ahead; indeed he called that they had arrived.

When Markus stepped behind the senior Knight he was placing an aged key into the solid oak door before them. He turned it once and stopped, faced Markus and said, "To what you are about to bear witness requires a quiet tongue and a hard trust."

The Marshal paused for his words to be weighed.

Then: "Are you ready, Sir Honour?"

Markus nodded once, hoping for open space.

The key turned twice more; the Marshal pushed: the passage continued but sharply to the right, and not forty paces ahead they ended their journey upon a balcony. It overlooked a chamber that sprawled the full mileage of the mighty fortress beneath its foundation. And what filled this voluminous expanse formed the myriad questions rushing into his mind.

Markus focused on the closest of the activity off to one side, which also captivated the Marshal: eight monks worked two identical large wooden devices in an area closest to Markus; several others nearby were hanging or inspecting hundreds of small pieces of parchment upon scores of thin ropes that crisscrossed above them.

Markus turned to the Marshal for an explanation, who held his eyes observant on the operation below. "Some of our brothers visited a far east people, from the 'City of a Thousand Bridges'— descendents in a patron house of the Magi and also the first Christian of that distant kingdom (such was their claim). They came back with this device. We call it a 'letter press': ink is applied to individual letters made of clay and pressed onto parchment. The Gospel testament possessed by Jacques, and then you, was one of its fruits." The Marshal looked at Markus, the pride in his eyes channelled into his voice. "The time will come when you will no longer be one of just dozens with the Words of our LORD to read and ponder."

Markus was not immediately impressed. "What good are books to the illiterate?"

The Marshal's eyes only grew brighter. "We will teach them," he replied. "We have already begun in the surrounding duchies, with success."

"Knights, teaching common folk to read...?" Markus was incredulous. "Most brothers are just as uneducated as the people. Those that are not are rightly tasked with the money-handling business, without which the whole of Europe would be at the mercy of the Lombards."

"I do not speak of Knights, but of clergy— bishops even."

"With the approval of the Curia?"

The Marshal turned from Markus to observe the labours going on below them. "In a manner of speaking. Let us say they shall not be in a position to object. Still, precautions are necessary; it is why we sought you out."

"The gospel book is no longer in my possession," said Markus. "It was lost at Cresson." He decided it was little use bringing up Percy; the brother was dead in any case.

"That *is* a pity," the Templar officer replied, and his sentiment was genuine.

Markus tried to read the face of the Marshal, but he turned to a set of stairs and proceeded down to the floor. What did he mean, "precautions"? Markus followed with an apprehensive inquiry: "You are planning an attack on the Church?" There was no immediate objection. "There will be war, and the Saracens will destroy the victor."

"Which is why the caliphates must cease to be a threat," he replied in a tense manner. He recomposed himself. "You will not see the move against the Curia in your lifetime, Sir Honour. But you may aid in its success."

"How?"

"Teach others as Jacques taught you."

"Why should my teaching be any different than that of the local priests? Are they not honourable men?"

The Marshal exhaled a loud breath. "Many are; speak to the shepherd of your own village if you feel so highly concerning him." The Marshal paused between several monks working on an agricultural project that flanked their path. "Many priests know little beyond the counsel of personal experience or what they modestly discern from the sermons they are given to read."

"And the Holy Father?"

The senior Templar moved along the path into an area of engineering unfamiliar to Markus, though it appeared to be for military employment. "Is he the Head of the Body..." the Marshal stopped and faced Markus, holding up a small book—a Gospel Testament similar to the one given him by his captain. "...or is the LORD Christ? Christendom existed without the See for six centuries; concerning bishops, the primacy of Rome is not affirmed in the writings of the Blessed Doctors Jerome or Gregory."

Markus turned his head back to the busy monks at the press. He did not have the knowledge of these authorities, and he did not like the caustic air of implied revolution. He looked back at the Testament, still grasped by the Marshal near the side of his leg, and a terrible thought surfaced. "All copies of the Vulgate are commissioned from Rome, and they speak with such confidence in the matter. Is it possible the Curia has altered the Word of our LORD to uphold the right claimed for the pope?"

The Marshal nodded as if he knew the conversation would proceed to this point. He turned with a beckon of his finger. Markus followed the Templar off the platform and down a side of stairs. At the bottom, his guide took a right and walked nearly a dozen broad steps to another oak door. He gave Markus a long gaze, then rapped his knuckles on the door three times; pause; two more raps in quick succession.

The door opened with barely a sound. Markus and his guide walked down three semi-circle steps to another door. The Marshal opened it and welcomed

Markus to go in before him: the room was more like a long corridor, barely wide enough for ten armoured men to stand shoulder-to-shoulder. A series of high-backed desks inside small partitioned alcoves lined one side of the room, leaving the remaining space for walking. Seated at these stations were monks, busily copying long scrolls to parchment or illuminating a page with the most tedious strokes. No head turned to regard the visitors—nothing about their postures so much as hinted that these men knew they were not presently alone.

Markus looked back to the Marshal, standing behind him; the man pressed Markus forward with a single nod. As he walked further on Markus saw that the room was actually crossed horizontally by another, larger chamber.

When Markus entered this area, his eyes were drawn to a large platform set back into an antechamber directly in front of him, giving the whole room a † shape. Within this small space sat a large open tome upon a gold-gilded marble lectern. Covering the wall above was a magnificent fresco of bold colours depicting Moses, Elijah, King David, Daniel, Jeremiah, Isaiah, The Four Evangelists, Peter, Paul, and James; in the centre and dominating was Christ Jesus in all His white-silver brilliance from the Transfiguration on the mount. The light from the candles and torches played across the faces, giving them a kind of life that made the hair on one's skin stand.

Markus's eyes descended back to the large weathered book and waited for the Marshal to explain the importance of what his eyes were seeing.

The officer's voice came in a reverent hush: "*Codex Alexandrinus.*"

Markus did not have the education to comprehend the great significance of this so the Marshal continued.

"In the early years of the Church, during the time when Saint Cyril was Patriarch of Alexandria, there arose a dispute between the Patriarch and the Alexandrian prefect involving a local pagan philosopher. It was discovered that she had a copy of the Jewish scriptures in a pagan temple. Cyril had the scrolls seized and the temple razed." The Marshal moved up to the codex and laid a careful hand upon it before continuing his lesson. "History is silent what became of the scrolls however a codex with his name in some fashion came to the church marking the Ascension of Christ, destroyed when the infidels took the Holy City from the Persians. After Jerusalem was freed by Godfrey, and our Order formed, one of the first missions of the new Templar Knights was to search the city and recover anything of value. Buried under the ruin of the Olivet chapel, they found this codex."

Markus's mind worked over these details. He knew that in the Templar officer's words was some deep meaning he should appreciate.

"It is in the Greek of antiquity, Sir Honour:

a copy of the Books of Moses and the Prophets, the Holy Gospels, and the Spirit-wrought words of the Apostles to the churches."

The pieces slid into place and clicked: there were many versions of the Vulgate located in larger churches. But being in Greek meant the codex came from a time when the Church was very young and Rome not yet the appointed centre of the Christian world. This revelation meant the Testament that Markus held in his possession, along with the copies being produced in the main chamber, were from second or third generation Greek texts at worst. But his concern still remained unaddressed: "And The Vulgate?"

The Marshal gave Markus an reassuring look. "By the grace of Holy God Rome has not been so bold as to compromise the Holy Writ." The Marshal stepped off the platform to make way for a monk wishing to consult the divinely inspired pages.

"Even so, by preserving Scripture and commentary in the legal dialect of the Holy Office, the ranking stewards of the Church have ensured they can teach how they wish without fear the laity will discern inconsistencies in their teachings. Just enough of the Gospel is veiled to keep the anvil of damnation swaying over Christendom, which is useful to pick the pockets of villagers and royal treasuries."

Markus frowned at the implication. "So what happens when parishioners with your testaments conclude the Church hierarchy is nothing but a thief, even a tyrant? You are not much among the commoner: they will not consider that perhaps their local shepherds are good and true; they will be stirred up—by opportunists—as ones unjustly abused. Good men and women—such as my sister and other noble lords, serving God as they have been called, will be harmed or perish. A different tyranny will emerge no better than the one you claim to oppose, and no easier to control."

The Marshal smarted at Markus's cynical tone. "Some bloodshed is unavoidable: Rome has chosen its own end by acting to spread our faith through domination of conscience and wealth."

Faltering beneath the weight of all this, Markus sat down on the lowest step of the lectern bearing the Integrity of the Faith. The Marshal followed him.

"Nothing is ever certain, beyond the LORD's victory accomplished for us. Even such steadfast confidence in achieving the everlasting realm through faith, *as God Himself promises us*, is called 'blasphemous' by many called to teach us; this must cease. Thus our Order shall risk the path set before it. We have always protected Christendom from the unbeliever; we are steward to her most Sacred History. We must continue in our Holy Mandate to protect the weak, to preserve Christendom in the Word of God, to give hope to the despairing, and prepare for when those who fear us decide the Banner of the Red Cross has outlived its purpose."

"To educate Christendom in an effort to reform

the Church is a noble cause, but to supplant the whole Papal court exceeds my mind! Are we even the best agents to initiate such a blessed task when our own Order struggles in temptation?"

The Marshal stiffened his back. "There comes a point when we must trust God's Holy Judgment on our works." He rose to his feet. "Before I leave you to your path, I would show you one thing more."

Markus got up and followed the Marshal to a private hall located by way of a hidden door cut into the stone of the chamber they were now occupying. Inside was a small Christian altar lined and flanked with white flowers.

"This is where we perform the sacrament of marriage, Sir Honour."

Markus spun on his heels, "The Pope would—".

"—condemn us." The Marshal bowed his head to determine the best way to explain the motive behind what Markus was seeing.

"Holy God commands man and woman to be fruitful and increase in the world, yet the Holy Father imposes chastity on the Sacred Orders because our LORD Himself took no wife. By what authority has he to order any man to be celibate when Christ made no such order, even of His own Apostles? Our LORD bore no sword, nor hoe: has He condemned making just war, or farming the land? Indeed, this vile law to bind that which God ordained has borne out lines of poor bastards that could fill a city; further, noble sons join our ranks to escape their duty as men of

God—they receive no protection against temptation, for they have rejected the antidote and the blessing of family, and have not the strength to persevere in trials for wife and child." Confidence in this plan was evident on the Marshal, both in posture and voice. "Our LORD expects great things in His name from the station he has granted to us. Return to your homeland, Sir Honour. Come back with the one that God desires for you and help us to forge the future. We especially need one such as you."

Little by little, the LORD of Creation was pulling in the line of his life, with him as the helpless fish. It was a fate that Markus had chosen, and God was right to let him suffer in this vision that had been presented.

But what did the Marshal mean: One such as him?

The Templar officer appeared confused for a moment at the inquiry. Then he proceeded to fill Markus in on details he had never been told: "Your father became a great patron of the Order when you chose to join us. We spoke by letter often; he told us many things of your birthright, possibly because he feared he would not have the opportunity; things a father does not tell a son until he is of an age to shoulder its weight."

Markus's brow furrowed at the strange turn in the dialogue. He watched the Marshal move to the back of the chapel and knock upon a door lightly. It cracked open; the Marshal spoke with someone out of sight on the other side.

He returned to Markus after the short conversation concluded and wordlessly motioned for him to take a position at the front pew and remain standing. The Marshal's eyes moved back to the doorway; Markus did likewise. He spared another look at the altar, noticing for the first time the golden arch, covered in lilies, that bent over the altar; in its centre was an empty hook. Behind the altar, the chancel opened into an apse. Gathered around its perimeter were seven wooden statues, lavishly painted as angels. The fresco that adorned the apse was a representation of a star-filled heaven, with one especially large, silver star fashioned to be especially prominent. At its apex, the heaven was torn open, and looking down was the face of Christ, shining like the sun, his wounded hands raised in a sign of peace.

Movement caught the edge of Markus's sight: a priest was entering the sanctuary at a deliberate pace; he swayed an incense burner back and forth, filling the chamber with a rich, pleasant aroma of fruit and spices. As he performed his task, a low form of the *Sanctus* rolled into the chapel from voices that might have been standing somewhere above.

A young monk dressed all in white followed in like manner and bearing an ornate silver seven-candle candelabrum, which he placed to the right side of the altar.

The chant transitioned to the *Agnus Dei*. Another monk, dressed in linen-white, entered carrying a silver platter with the same measured steps as his brothers. He placed the dish just to the right of centre near the candelabrum.

The choir of male voices shifted to the *Crucifixis*. The priest that entered next was dressed in purple; he carried a Spear, which produced a frightful image if it was not some trick of the dim light: a great drop of blood appeared about to drop from its tip, but it did not! The cleric hung the Spear from the hook Markus had perceived at the centre of the arch so that the wavering blood drop hovered just above the altar.

The chanting grew in volume, and several voices shifted to represent a complete octave, enriching the chant with its expanded and complex degrees of rhythm and meter.

Three more clerics now entered: a priest dressed in scarlet with one monk in front and another behind. The monk bore a chalice covered with a white veil. Light—just barely contained—appeared to be emanating from inside the vessel. When it was placed on the altar, the veil was removed and a great bead of blood fell into the chalice, followed by two others.

Markus's body was trembling; he dropped to his knees and refused to look upon the altar, for he felt stripped of all clothing and flesh, and less than worthy to behold such a supernal event any longer: *How have I come into such divine grace that I should be allowed a glimpse upon the rite of The Holy Grail?*

After several moments he dared to raise his eyes: the celebrant dressed in purple was looking at him; he pointed first to his eye and then to the Blessed Grail: the priest was calling Markus to come to the table and gaze into the Sacred Vessel. As the chanters moved to *Quem Quaeritis* Markus found himself compelled forward, his body shaking with every step like a tree in mid-autumn buffeted by the first cold north winds.

When he was standing before the table, the celebrant in scarlet picked up the Grail and placed it beneath Markus's bowed head so that Markus could glimpse at the contents.

"LORD, I am not worthy. Have mercy..." Markus whispered.

Pure silver Light poured into Markus's eyes: he was blind, but he heard hammers, agonised screams of pain and the cry "Father, forgive them!", the most terrible peals of thunder, the sound of heavy fabric torn asunder, the cracking and rolling of stone; in the Light Markus thought he heard the distant singing of a multitude, perceived the barest outlines of three Faces—a hand came into view, its wrist bore a grievous puncture; Markus thought he heard the words, "for the remission of sins".

The Light vanished; the Grail was no longer before him. Markus cast his eyes about the room but saw no one but himself and the Marshal, now standing.

"It was a vision then," Markus said.

The Marshal shook his head: "Look upon the altar, and know the truth."

Markus did so and saw the candelabrum still in its place where it was set down. Upon the linen were two round impressions: one where the Platter had been sitting, and the other where The Holy Grail of the Passion had been: it had been no mere vision.

Markus placed a hand over his eyes; his face was wet, possibly from the brilliant Light, but just as likely he had been weeping. Markus retreated from the altar and returned to the side of the Templar senior officer.

"What did you see?"

Markus opened his mouth but found he did not have the words, he would never have them. "I cannot speak it. I would have given up my spirit if I could." He gazed at the Marshal. "What did you see?"

The officer's face became forlorn. "I cannot tell you, for I have never been invited to gaze into the Cup of Christ."

"How come I was given this great invitation? I am no Perceval; indeed I am hardly worthy to be a server at the Round Table."

"How can you say you are unworthy?" the Marshal replied with an edge. "The Grail does not err in calling those to partake of its sacred gifts. If the Cup marks you as worthy, then you are worthy. It is a grievous mockery of our crucified and risen LORD to say you are not what He has declared you are."

The rebuke cut Markus to the heart. "Forgive my offense, lord Marshal."

"It is forgiven you, Sir Honour. You understand now just what this Order possesses. You see now why we chose to wear the Red Cross with white or black tunic after Sir Perceval le Rouge, the Grail Knight who bore these colours and device upon his shield."

Markus very much wanted to know how the Templars had come upon these Holy Vessels, and their heritage.

"The two brothers that founded this Order discovered the Grail, along with the Platter and Candelabrum of the Seven Churches buried beneath the floor of Saint Peter's at Antioch. The Spear had been found by a soldier of the first great pilgrimage led by Godfrey when that host were under siege and nearly depleted of all hope. Truly, the Spear revealed itself; it was carried before the army and the Saracens, who outnumbered the Christians greatly, were routed—our scribes testify the army was aided by a heavenly host. Godfrey received the Spear, and the other sacred tokens of our LORD's passion and revelation with humble thankfulness; yet he could not risk these blessed artefacts remaining in the Land of Christ to be captured, and so they were secreted to this fortress." The Marshal's voice grew now with sincere excitement. "What greater sign than these that the True Cross awaits our rescue, that restoration of the Kingdom of God on earth will surely come to pass? That the Blessed Order of the Temple has been chosen as His instrument to accomplish this? ...With Jerusalem, and the Holy Artefacts marching again among God's armies, all of Christendom will be greater than Arthur's Logres!"

Markus appreciated his superior's enthusiasm. Even so, his Templar brothers needed to know their plans would fail if they continued to yield to temptations. Perhaps that is also why God had led him to this point, had granted him the privilege to gaze into the Grail: to be a herald of His rebuke so that the Order might succeed. What else could be the meaning of his having heard one of the seven Blessed Words of the Cross: 'Father, forgive them, for they know not what they do.'

Markus was overcome with the thought that Holy God would see fit to use him in this capacity, in spite of all Markus's failings. And he would not fail the Almighty in this calling. "Lord Marshal, I was weaned on the romance of the Grail, for it was Arthur that defeated and acted as a divine means of the conversion of my House. He chose the founder of our House, the Blessed Sir Bunian, to be a part of his Round Table of Christian Knights. When the Sacred Cup appeared to the Table upon that Feast of Pentecost it was not a time for celebration but bittersweet despair: Arthur had been told that when the Grail appeared, and the quest to achieve it completed, that the Grail would be removed from Logres and his realm would crumble beneath the weight of its self-service, its increasing unbelief, and its incessant civil war. And it was so. Milord: The Grail was not found by our brothers; The Grail revealed itself. It is a sign that a portion of us will soon have the Gospel of Christ taken from our sight. We will be made blind—stumbling in darkness; thirsting—like parched land without rain for many seasons. If the exceptional realm of Logres was not spared, with all its brave Knights and charitable deeds through Christian faith, what new devil's folly is it that we conclude the Grail's presence means for us great glory? Indeed, for hearkening to our own deceptive voices, calling this 'wisdom'... for testing the LORD in our warring with each other and destroying tenuous peace accords to satiate our depraved passions... for hearts made hard against the grace of Holy God, and taking from crushed spirits the gratuitous mercy and sure hope of immortality won by our LORD: for choosing this evil and walking in this darkness the Grail comes to declare such as these shall be cut off and cast out. His Righteous Hand is surely in Outremer; we are given to our enemies as the rebellious, unthankful Hebrews were given over to theirs. Milord, I have borne witness to it. I justly feel His Rod upon my back for my transgression, and the resulting sins..." Markus felt the pang of disappointment that he perceived crossing the Marshal's demeanour.

"The Grail was taken away. And yet here it is!"

"Indeed—to demonstrate God's fervent desire to grant us mercy, is it here! The LORD is never changing in His purpose: to call His people to repent.

We have tread from the Narrow Path."

Markus watched as the Marshal pondered his words deeply. The longer he watched the Templar officer the more Markus felt what little hope there was to influence his superior become nil. It was too difficult to turn from a course where so much had already been set in motion.

"Perhaps your wariness is true. Others should hear these words you speak, that your Order may better weigh all things."

"You have the words from me, that you may find an audience who will heed your rank."

The Marshal looked distressed. "The Holy Chalice did not consider my rank when it gave you its vision. The Grail of our LORD has chosen you and none other can deliver its images."

"I am truly sorry, milord: I cannot tarry. God has pressed another, more urgent task upon my heart."

The Templar pressed his lips in disappointment, but accepted the decision. "You are welcome to join us, Sir Honour, when you believe you are ready. Can we count on your sword?"

What the Marshal wanted was nothing short of rebellion, but violence against the Church would not cleanse her of the waywardness that only increased the more her caretakers plunged directly into the affairs of monarchs and armies. How would this change with the Templars pulling the strings instead of worldly cardinals and bishops? He could say as much, but the Marshal was unlikely to hear;

many cogs and wheels were already turning to ends of which the officer spoke and alluded; a wary voice could only expect to be crushed by placing himself in their path.

"I pray that our Order might be successful in the quest it has laid out for its members and Christendom. It is on this hope, and upon fervent prayer, that I *implore* the Order not to suffer the poison in our body, nor to take up the sword against brothers and sisters of the faith. Trust in God's will, embrace His call to charity and brotherhood, heed not to the desires of baseness or whimsy: to this purpose I affirm that you have my blade and voice to the last drop of my lifeblood."

The Marshal embraced Markus's arm with a firm hand and warm countenance. Then the ranking Templar handed him a roll of worn parchment: "Upon this you will find information concerning the history of your House, as written in the hand of your father. It was passed to us by the Preceptor of Templecombe, where you were trained. Guard well that noble sword, for it has surely been wielded by hands worthy of aspiration: this the present Preceptor himself has said. Now, go with the blessing of God and your Poor Brothers, sir Knight, and fulfil His will for you."

VIII : again, the land of christ

After Hattin, Saladin moved against Jerusalem and other bastions of Christendom, until Christian Outremer consisted wholly of a collection of scattered feudal holdings, mainly upon the coast and nearby. After the loss of Jerusalem and Acre, the port city of Tyre was raised to prominence; indeed the defences of the *de facto* capital had yielded the relentless advance of Saladin.

A wave rocked Markus on the rigging, the movement causing a beam from the sun approaching the horizon to squint his eye. The shadows bathed the great stronghold in supernal golds and solemn purples. Tyre had grown wealthy through its centuries-old textile trade; the thick ramparts and high towers exuded what its vast riches could afford.

When the ship docked in its berth, Markus made for the pseudo-capital of the western Christian world. People shuffled all around him; he spotted the White Crosses of Hospitallers but none of his Order. Markus's pulse beat a more rapid pace to match his gait: Would Ridefort slip through his grasp again?

Would God grant him this quarry as a merit, a stone that would surely tip the balance in his favour before his being summoned to the eternal court?

A quick question to patrol guardsman yielded frustrating information: Guy was still alive and king; he and the men attached to his person had been denied entrance to Tyre for almost a year; Guy and the highest ranking Templars (meaning Ridefort) were marching south, probably to Acre; they had left not two days hence.

Markus was glad he had chosen not to adorn the mantle of his Order outside of Europe, else he would not have gotten past the gates for the mount and provisions he needed for his new road. Besides, the colours beneath his face might connect him to 'Sir Honour', a name that could find him trouble and detour his path.

He picked up a strange yellow fruit the like he had never seen, even as his mind wandered to the task before him. The road to Acre was easy enough to follow given his previous service in the Land. From the early morrow, it would take at least a full day of nearly unbroken riding before Markus should expect to see anyone from the military cavalcade, *if* the time of departure provided him was accurate. Markus placed the fruit back. He could waste very little time with trifles if he wanted to catch the army before it organised at Acre, for Ridefort would then be impossible to engage.

"I am happy to find the LORD has willed you

safely to this city, Markus."

He turned to the voice, but Markus provided no immediate visible reaction upon seeing Charle the Hospitaller leaning against a building close-by.

"Good day, sir" Markus responded evenly. "Good day, Charle. It is my prayer God would see me to the threshold of the Holy Sepulchre."

"All will be revealed in time, no doubt." Charle pushed off the building toward Markus. "Come; take respite from your journey. I shall acquire you food and shelter." He lowered his voice to a whisper.

Markus followed the Hospitaller to the inn where Charle had been staying for the last several days; Markus learned that the Knight had been prepared to wait for him for up to a month. He did not know to what he owed such a gesture as this. Markus proceeded to show his appreciation over a dinner on his purse. During the course of the meal, the Hospitaller provided him the news of a world very different than what Markus had known: namely Christian kingdoms pushed to the brink.

Guy de Lusignan was still king—a king without a capital while the Egyptian caliphate controlled Jerusalem. Guy had been released by Saladin soon after Hattin as a show of respect among equals. There was little about Guy that would worry a skilled military commander; it was Guy's capriciousness and Ridefort's pride that had given the Saracen world its prize. Under the guise of honour, it was practical for the sultan to discover which Christian city-jewel the monarch would hand over next. Moreover, Guy had plenty of strong opposition inside and outside his court. Therefore, to a shrewd Saladin, Guy's presence could provide another political crisis such as the one that led to Christendom's undoing at Hattin.

One of the opposed was Conrad of Montefferat. Little was known about his pedigree in the ranks (for the Templars had always been sworn to the king of Jerusalem). It *was* known that Lord Conrad was one of few to hand Saladin a rare defeat—this just as he was given the command to a besieged Tyre preparing to capitulate to Allah's banners. After the grave losses following Guy's first full year of reign, Conrad publicly challenged Guy for the crown. Tyre was equal to Jerusalem in all respects concerning economic, geographical, and strategic values. But Conrad lacked political leverage; with Guy backed by the Templars and King Richard of England no man could easily take the ranking throne and sceptre in Outremer from him. And if the Templars still supported Guy, this could only mean—

"Ridefort." Markus spat the name out like drawn serpent poison.

Charle looked at him with more than curiosity. "You speak of him as one bearing a trespass against you?"

Markus pushed away the remainder of the morsels that sat on his plate; his appetite was fleeting. "Have you heard of Cresson?"

Charle bristled. "Indeed; I was there. We lost

a great Master in that battle: Roger Moulins. Your Ridefort barely escaped with his life—the only survivor as the account is written."

Markus ripped off a piece of bread and placed it in his mouth. "He is the devil's, maybe; not mine." He chewed the bread with more purpose than the food deserved. "Anyway, there was another survivor of that unholy massacre not in the initial accounts." Charle flicked his eyes to Markus and likely considered the manner in which the bread was being disintegrated; he understood. "Sir Jacques taught me much of war, and how to employ with honour and our LORD Christ in our hearts." The anguish at Christendom's loss of such a fine captain, and the man Markus considered his spiritual father, rose up to drown him. He needed air, and sought it in the late watch of the night, atop the nearest rampart.

Charle followed, and after allowing a few hundred feet of time to pass in silence he said, "One should be surprised that the Temple Master would go through such pains to lead a massacre of his own Christian brethren. But then there are persistent whisperings."

"Eh?"

"He was captured at Hattin, along with Guy, Reynald de Châtillon, and the Master of Ibelin. As you know, Knights of our order—"

"—are not allowed to keep their lives." Markus became silent, and looked out over the flat moon-swept wilderness. The Hospitaller Master, Moulins, had never been a friend of Guy or Gerard. In protest, he had refused to hand over his key to the chest containing the king's crown when Guy was crowned (indeed it was told that he threw the key from a tower). His politics were his death sentence. Sir Jacques likewise, who threatened to censure, before the Outremer nobility and the Curia, key allies of Guy. Moreover, by nature of their vocations, both men came to know much of the mind of Ridefort, thus both men may have paid for such as well: the Templar Master was known to strike deals that served his ends—be they rival Christian Houses, Persians, the Byzantines, or Muslims. If Saladin spared his life at the Horns, it was because he made it invaluable. "I must retire for the night. I have a hard ride on the morrow."

Charle placed a hand upon his arm. "You go after Ridefort? He will kill you if he discovers your identity. If he is capable of sending beloved Christians to the Almighty, we know not what hellish arrangements he has made to escape death at the hands of the caliphate. And what of Percy's message?"

"The Holy Sepulchre will be no less a ruin in a fortnight or even a season, and no path to its door is yet delivered to me. In the meanwhile, a vision has come upon me, quickened by the news you bring; an immediate purpose to act as his sword-arm for which our good LORD has led me back to this place. I am compelled to see it through if but for the chance of feeling a breath's worth of satisfaction from the

Maker of heaven and earth."

The steady jade eyes of the Hospitaller spoke more than lips ever could: Markus perceived that Charle disapproved, deeply, but the Knight uttered not a word as Markus descended the stair in the near-darkness.

IX : duel of wills

Markus set out after the morning Mass. He kept a decent pace for nearly two days, sleeping lightly on his horse and dismounting as often as he could to save the animal's strength. Awake or asleep, his training kept him alert for any movement from an attempted ambush. He had no purses of gold, the supplies he carried were clear, and it was a public road. He expected no trouble.

A large portion of the third day expired before Markus saw the first hint of the rear columns and the contingent of servants. Just as the first stars were brightening their fires in the cobalt expanse, Markus overtook a Templar—a sergeant according to his brown tunic and Red Cross upon the shoulder. Sergeants were men of the Order who possessed no birthright; they would never be Knights, but they provided a stout backbone. There was motivation to serve well, for there were high stations in the Order a sergeant could achieve.

Markus donned the iconic garb of the Order and introduced himself to the Templar sergeant, indicating an pressing need of an audience with the Master, Ridefort. He did his best to suppress the urgency in his voice, which might come off as suspicious.

The man gave him a look of one trying to deduce Markus's unspoken business, and whether such a random unknown man could be trusted: 'Why would a Templar Knight appear out of the desert, days after the host had departed?'—a fair question. Finally he shrugged, mumbling something to the effect that he had not seen the Master.

It was possible he was telling the truth; Ridefort spent most of his time with his advisors, far from the rear of the army. Even so, the sergeant would know Ridefort's location, or would have a superior who did.

"My business with the Master is personal in nature." Markus indicated a patch of desert by a group of rocks some hundred yards back up the road: "I will keep to my camp when you muster in the morning." Markus reached beneath his tunic, found his Templar signet ring. "Give the Master this. Tell him a ghost from Cresson haunts him on this road. He will reward you." The countenance of the sergeant brightened at the thought of so easy an earned reward.

Markus retreated to make camp several hundred feet away, to prepare his soul to receive a measure of absolution, and thank God for the honour to remove a blight from the Body of Christ.

An armoured foot to his stomach ended Markus's slumber. It was not yet daybreak, but there was enough light to see Ridefort, the wicked smile creasing on his face.

"So your cowardice caught up with you in that Saxon sty of human refuse. Now you would slay me to regain what putrid honour you may have possessed," said the Templar Master.

"Only your arrogance would convince you that I returned to this holy land solely to take your head. I am but a pilgrim here; rather a pilgrim than a spineless dog who ravishes his own brothers, leads them to their death to keep secret his lying with the unbeliever in the shadows."

Hellish fire lighted in Ridefort's eyes, they were like molten steel.

"Jacques was like kin to you. You will meet him before the sun rises. Then your country will be despoiled to my content; *every* heart that has loved your wretched head, *every* soul that has given you quarter, *every* eye that has seen you shall join you *in hell*."

Markus took hold of Audacit'in Domino and cast away the sheath. "If the end of my mortal body be now, I go with joy, to be rid of this world; if a prayer still be in your soul, use it this hour to beg God's mercy. As for the eyes and souls and hearts of which you speak: my death or yours, either will put an end to the curse I have laid on them, for God will surely preserve them according to His rich grace."

The Master secured the coif on his head, then pulled his own sword to the ready. Ridefort moved to action, making small circles with the tip in the warming dawn air. Markus followed him, his blade raised and steady.

Ridefort's first strike was meant to be parried, the strong vibration on Markus's blade meant to be heard and felt.

Markus positioned his blade neck-high. The next attack was like the first but harder and also meant to send a message of arrogant superiority, that the sword's wielder would be relentless.

The third attack from the Master truly began the duel; it was a searching attack meant to gauge strength and reveal initial weakness in form. Markus had none of the latter: teaching the men of Audaciter Deus—peasant and soldier alike—was as much for him as it was for them. Markus decided he would counter the next attack. There was no reason to give Ridefort confidence or a chance to reveal an unknown weakness.

The Master assailed him with a cut, diagonal and vicious from shoulder to waist; Markus caught the blade midway through its course, directing it down to the sand. While Ridefort was forced to follow the momentum, Markus placed his blade on a line to slice.

The Templar Master lurched his torso away from the point and brought his sword to the ready from its parried position; the movement was awkward and Markus used the moment to make some weak thrusts hoping on chance that his enemy would guess wrong.

He did not. Instead the Master retreated with sure steps, alerting Markus to a vulnerability it was right to dread: Ridefort had fought hundreds of duels in the unpredictability of shifting sand, but for Markus it had been years since he had been tested on such terrain. The trick was to never plant a foot solid; the weight turned a foot sideways, buckling the knee, often causing one to land prostrate—a sure death.

Markus moved forward and tried a blow to the head that the Master pushed away; two cuts to each shoulder yielded no quick answers; the fight would have to be taken closer, where Markus could use his adversary's weight against him. The fact Markus was a good fifty pounds lighter meant that he was less susceptible to the ground even after granting his opponent experience: proficiency was nothing when forced to bad footing.

Markus looped into a more guarded stance and let his eyes flash a cockiness he did not feel.

Ridefort took the bait and came in with a strong thrust; Markus twisted and shifted his sword to guard a backswing while he came about. The two swords met; Ridefort pressed on the flat of his blade hoping to push Markus to his knees. Markus gave him what he wanted, for a moment, then released the pressure from the top half of his sword.

Ridefort's weapon slid against Markus's and

off at the tip; the Master's full weight caused him to stumble past, but he did not fall.

Not waiting to regain balance, Ridefort attacked with a primal scream that sent Markus stumbling; stability regained the Master kept on his new advantage with several hard blows that Markus found hard to block, parry, retreat from.

A charge from Ridefort ended with a one-handed strike that Markus dodged but put his sword out of attack position. The attack ended close to Markus—close enough for the Master to raise his shoulder into Markus's chest. The brute assault forced away Markus's breath; the physical attack was not followed up allowing Markus to two-hand his weapon in a rigid vertical position.

Despite this apparent reprieve Markus was panting hard, revealing the cunning purpose of Ridefort's attack: Markus was skilled, but his enemy had discerned he was out of sorts with the elements.

Markus attacked with a down stroke that would have gouged Ridefort's sword arm, a parry would at the least weaken its strength; the attack was blocked and countered with an upward blow aimed at Markus's face; blocked, and Markus was attacking again now; blocked; Markus spun on his feet, took a cut at the knees that was pushed through by Ridefort's blade, tilting Markus forward. He was losing control. In desperation Markus pushed with all his might forward, his shoulder winning its mark upon Ridefort's knees, locking them up. With a grunt, Ridefort pitched forward and fell.

Markus was in a better position having landed on his hands and knees, save that Audacit'in Domino was out of sight; he looked fast about hoping to catch its glimmer in a beam of breaking sun.

Spit entered his eyes instead. Markus tried to blink away the rude attack of malice, but hundreds of grains splashed his vision. They thickened quickly in the spittle around Markus's sockets; those in his eyes grated his lids to a near-close; tears were no help as his sight was reduced to a gritty prison.

A harsh boot to his side rolled him over; another rolled him again. A soft thud in the sand somewhere nearby was a dirty taunt; even if he could grasp the heirloom sword it would find no mark while he fought blindness and lack of breath.

Pointed metal met his cheekbone followed by sharp rap to the back of the head. Markus knew he was fading; shadows and light were all his blinded vision could create but he tried to push himself off the ground anyway. He heard a voice, but it may as well have been a foreign tongue in his ringing ears. A well-aimed attack, blunt and hard, came to his stomach. Markus thought he would retch. He gasped and coughed, inviting air that could not come fast enough; when it did, it was with tasteless desert. He gagged and rolled to his back. His head pounded and edged his vision.

A fierce kick to the side of his head made it complete.

X : a second duel of wills

The smell of incense was sweet and exotic—nothing like the earthy aroma used by the priests in rugged England. Markus sat upright, doing his best to shake the intoxicating effects of the fragrance from invading his senses completely.

The room was dark, hazy; torchlight obscured by half-drawn curtains hanging from the ceiling and around the bed cast a flickering dull-yellow upon the room. His bed was not quite in the centre, confirmed by a strong desert breeze that caressed his exposed skin.

His shirt hung loose over the bandages he was now beginning to sense from his sudden movement. Markus dodged his eyes left and right looking for Audacit'in Domino. He found it leaning on a chair very close to him (out of arm's reach), where also hung his shirt, tunic and travel sack. His hosts were confident in the blend of head injury and spice—and with fair reason: Markus looked upon his blade like a posy of Criststar lilies.

A door opened; the brightness of day spilled

in and the scented clouds swirled like angry spirits.

The figure that entered was refined, even in what must have been his casual dress. His dark face was hidden with ease inside of Markus's room; the shadows played on his features so that he could have been a demon from the underworld of his religion. The Arab pulled a chair for himself to sit; when he was comfortable he provided an hospitable gaze on Markus with a greeting in the name of their god, *Allah*. His accent was harsh on Markus's language, no doubt learned in order to do business with the Franks. (To the understanding of Muslims, all Christians were "Franks"—a reference to the old Frankish empire that was not long in the West past the sons of Charlemagne.)

Markus offered no reply to the greeting; it was best to discover his host's intentions. His host deduced as much and called over his shoulder in his own tongue. A man-servant appeared with speed bearing a platter of bread, water, and fruit unknown to Markus. The tray was placed on Markus's lap, a bite and sip was taken from each of the refreshments to prove their lack of poison, and then the servant took his leave with a bow to his master.

Markus was thankful for the nourishment that stared at him and thanked the LORD for its presence; he ate with discipline, taking his eyes from the Muslim only long enough to grab a chunk of bread.

"It seems that you are not loved by your own brothers," the Arab intoned. "It was my caravan that saved you from the death blow."

Markus blinked and understood what his role was to be—or at least the role the Arab hoped he would play. "The battle was personal in its nature and not an indication of failed loyalty to the Church or our cause in this land. My thanks to you, but it is the grace of Holy God that has truly delivered me."

The shadow of a smile quickly faded from the Saracen's lips. "I have traded much wealth to Franks in exchange for information."

Markus shrugged. "It was the will of Holy God that you should know what you bought."

The smile crawled back onto the Arab's countenance and he nodded. "We are of a mind, Christian." Markus's host stood from his seat. "You will be fit to travel tomorrow. What is your road?"

"Jerusalem, if its gates will receive me," replied Markus.

"They will not receive you in peace without the blessing of Allah. I may grant you this if you can tell me the destination of the army on the road."

Markus pushed away his food. "I know not their road, nor purpose. Neither are mine." The merchant gave a bow of his head in a manner that suggested he did not believe Markus. He watched as the merchant's eyes considered a machination churning in his mind.

Finally the Saracen said, "Perhaps the man who bested you may find the justice of a sword—even if it be the sword of an enemy. This would come to pass...if we knew the intent of his command."

"I cannot presume again upon the justice of God," Markus responded, genuine contrition in his voice. "If my enemy is meant to see the edge of a sword, I pray that it is mine. If it is to be otherwise, then God will lead my enemy to his path of destruction in His own time. I will not hasten this judgment by gaining favour with your people. The LORD has called me to this land to retrieve a message in the Place of Christ's Holy Death and Blessed Resurrection. His calling is my assurance I will complete this course."

Markus perceived his host was unwilling to place a man of contrary faith in Jerusalem without good reason, if not gain.

"I detect that you do not recognise the claim of my people on Jerusalem, to make such an arrogant request; malice is the bitter, but necessary fruit of disrespect."

Markus laughed. "I do not desire the new course of this conversation. I serve the only God of heaven and earth, and you serve the Allah of your prophet. We disagree about the superiority and value of our faith upon this world, our peoples square armies upon this battle-line, therefore I stake no private quarrel upon it."

The merchant crossed his arms. "This is my house. I will have an answer."

Markus sighed. "You ask respect and grant none of your own. What is the city to your people, other than one less city in the hands of the Christian?"

It was the Arab's turn to bear the mantle of scepticism. "The reverse of this is not in your own motives for making war in this land?"

Markus shook his head. "Nay. For centuries before now Christendom reckoned to fight each other for the vast wealth of vined hills, glittering fortresses, and sprawling farmlands. This wealth and beauty all still exist and are worth defending. What is here but scorched wasteland and parched river beds? The kingdom of heaven is not the greater or lesser by its presence or lack thereof in Christendom."

"Indeed; what is here for the Franks?"

"The city is where the Word of God comes alive for pilgrims," said Markus. "Also, despite that I cannot comprehend it, many folk serve the world here in noble stations to which they have been called. These all have a right to be defended."

The Arab leaned forward, ready to answer despite that Markus had made no inquiry. "The butchery that you Franks have wreaked upon the Muslim needs an equal response—taking *Al-Quds* is always the answer."

Markus crooked his neck at the words. "What of the souls laid to waste—Christian, Jew, and Arab— when the sons of Allah decided the East was theirs in the centuries past? And when this ceased to quench the thirst of your forebears and brother caliphs, you turned your gaze West. A few of those under the blessed protection of God, by way of *Audaciter-Deus* in my homeland, had ancestors that were sword-arms in

Touraine when a great army of your people, thinking they could march across Christendom from Iberia, were doubly thwarted by Charlemartel—the one your histories may call 'the Hammer', if they have the good sense to speak of him."

The Saracen merchant gave Markus a dangerous look. Markus returned the glance equally. He had been judged and challenged as an inferior in all respects. Perhaps the merchant thought him a Christian whose heart would tremble before an adversary, or whose resolve in God could be compromised for the sake of pleasantries. His host had commanded an answer, and to this Markus would be obedient.

"Beginning with Hagar the maidservant, and her son—who was bereft of the birthright of Abraham, you are a covetous and contentious people. You have no identity but the devil's, who through your great pride has long incited your lust for blood and the flesh. You strip the land before you like locusts and assimilate the wealth of nations as deceiver-princes. You demonstrate the pretence of good-will and proper manners, even allowing a person to believe what he will so long as you remain the temporal lord, but you are false: you do not allow Christians to gather in public, you bar the way to our holy sites—when you leave them standing—against those who seek only to pray and worship in peace, and any who confess Christ or deny your prophet are swiftly killed. Even your own have confessed to preferring the rule of the Frank to that of your own masters." Markus wondered if the boldness rising in his chest was the Spirit of God, as felt by the blessed martyrs before their final confessions of word and deed. "Your people burn with fire at the rivers of spilt blood of our first campaign against Jerusalem, just as we burn with fire for the seas of Christian blood rising from Castile to Constantinople to this land. Jerusalem is yours, because God wills it. He is taking His wayward House to account. And if he deals so justly with us—His own people by the blood of Jesus Christ—ponder with care what is stored up for such as yourselves."

"You speak as no Christian I have met. Your words are an insult, expecting me to believe that Franks do not seek the blood and wealth of Muslims, and to conquer the cities Allah has declared for himself. Your enemies will rejoice in this folly, and I will take satisfaction in offering up one such as you, *Insha'Allah*."

The Saracen rose from his chair, leaving the seat in its place. He made a motion with his hand, to someone Markus could not see. A man came to stand by his host within moments. Both spoke quickly in their tongue, and then referenced what Markus perceived to be a map, which the man who just entered had brought with him. The merchant nodded finally and his companion left in haste.

When the Muslim reached the door, he paused before exiting, then turned his head to Markus: "Rest well. You will join our convoy on the morrow's evening."

XI : the curse of jonah

The Saracens were as pious a people as any Christian in history; they battled and conquered, struggled and lost, praised and grieved. If salvation and the rewards of heaven were distributed solely on the merits of reverent and vigorous piety the Muslim might well dominate the highest levels of the supernal realm. The very being of Allah was in their blood, and they would spill theirs and others' in the pursuit to prove their belief. The Arabs understood the stakes of faith; knew that only one true religion could exist in any life, mortal or immortal. Markus honoured this view, thus he did not underestimate this foe.

It was not for the Christian to convert a man with the point of a sword. Those such as Markus were called to fight the Saracen lest he go unchecked in his drunken thirst for blood; the centuries past proved nothing less than this.

Therefore it was put forth: if nobles and kings would focus on the eradication of the infidel from

Christian lands—to the glory of God, in thanks for the Great Atonement of the Christ, to secure one's salvation and increase one's standing before Holy God—then they would be less interested in tormenting their own, conscripting Christian men to war against Christian men for Christian land.

Let the Church unite; let there be peace; let there be an answer to the unremitting incursions of the Saracen and the Moor upon Christian shores and against innocent peoples!

Christendom agreed: For if it was blood that the Christian world sought there was plenty within fifty miles of every home; the centuries had borne this out to be true—and truly how grievous. If it was wealth that was craved, there was plenty too that a Christian could plunder, wealth possessed by other Christians in much closer realms if such would be the aim.

Nay, not one Christian man would travel through months of starvation, disease, the most damnable weather just to fulfil base desires a world away.

Also cities required great numbers to seize and defend; not nearly enough could afford the great price of beasts, servants, food, or gear to take up arms for the banners of the Stitched Cross. It was a blessing of God that the kingdoms of Outremer could defend what they now possessed—and this through no small feat of wise governing, urgent diplomacy, accords with Jew and Muslim alike, and thanksgiving that the sons of Allah warred often among themselves seeking out Christian rulers for alliance.

Nay, nay it was not wealth or power that occupied the thoughts of many a Christian soldier and knight: they fought for the freedom of all to live and worship in peace and safety in this place from predators and tyrants, no matter their station; they fought for the opportunity of a life in a land a bit higher and more meaningful than a grimy existence from swaddling clothes to burial garments beneath the fickle gaze of fops; they endured all hardships, and risk of possessions, to journey in this faraway realm because this was where Christ had healed the infirm, was murdered on the Blessed Tree by the transgression and iniquities of Adam and all his descendents, then raised to life in the greatest Victory achieved: the LORD Jesus Christ accomplished none of this in Canterbury, Paris, Barcelona, or Rome.

But pride and avarice were bitter waters flowing from the depths of hell. The devil laboured hard to see spoiled fruit, watered by those poisoned currents, come from seeds planted by men. Whatever the primary good intents, whatever the integrity of individual men, the Christian armies had long fallen into the same pit with the Hebrews. And as He had done with them, Holy God appeared to be turning His face from Christendom with each new march. It could be perceived with each former city of Outremer who gazed up and saw the banners of the Saracen unfurled and clapping over their churches.

Such Christians were trapped in a purgatory more real than any preached by a church. All that was left was for these souls to sacrifice all their wealth, their aspirations, and find a way back to the West to pass away their final years; or they could hope for the chance to fight, to die for the faith and for freedom from their spiritual oppressors. For in these struggles was the hope that God would find these sacrifices acceptable, thereby meriting a place on the eternal shores closer to that final glory.

Markus was wrecked upon purgatorial shores of his own, accomplishing what he could to bathe in the divine Rays of Light. Perhaps the willing sacrifice he pursued was too easy: Ridefort had engaged in much regular battle, Markus had not. Perhaps God did not care that Markus was now ready for his life to be ended. Therefore, all Markus could do was continue to seek out just causes, until the Divine Master allowed sword or infirmity to claim him.

When the caravan was ready to leave, Markus was permitted his gear (the sword was to remain sheathed unless direct permission was given to wield it) and granted a diminutive mount (of the kind reserved for pregnant or aged women, for no Christian could be seen as an equal to a Muslim); he would ride with the servants at the back.

As the procession made its way to the southern horizon where Jerusalem waited, Markus found the small Christian token that he had hidden against his breast when the Saracens had been scurrying about, making ready the convoy. As he caressed its borders he reflected on his homeland, on the evening of his leave-taking...

'Was it in your plans to leave this noble raiment behind?'

Markus broke from his final preparations to address the feminine voice that so often assailed his defences with success.

'I do not go on this journey as a Knight of the Temple.'

'I would have you wear it, milord.'

Markus paused, nearly told her that bearing the Red Cross would bring attention to his person he was not prepared to meet. Instead he checked his measure of provisions.

'The Cross upon your heart will give you strength, or at least those around you who share your faith," Mairín said.

Markus turned, placed a hand on hers with affection, and pushed the Templar mantle back towards her. 'I am afraid that the state of my faith is not one I am proud to display in connection with the Cross of Christ. I am troubled, Mairín...troubled that God would forgive my iniquity but not allow me to forget. And now God would call me from this life—the very life I was rebuked to have abandoned, to which I have returned in penitence and humility? The life I should have desired from birth and truly desire now to honour my Father; which separates my mind from my burden? There is meaning in this I must discover.' Mairín's sweet face filled his eyes; her smile was warm and inviting; eyes that reflected the joy of the sun and the magic of the moon; a blend of fervent youth and unceasing grace to comprise a woman strong in mind, true in heart, upright in body, steadfast in love for God. Indeed, a Christian lady.

Mairín pressed the article back towards him. 'Keep this robe. Perhaps a time will come when you will seek it to cover your despair.'

Truly: a Christian Lady. 'If it makes your heart content, milady.' If he had not spoken he would have wept. He reached into the folds of his coat and pulled out a small roll of parchment. He had intended to give it to the guard at the gate with an order to pass it to Mairín before she retired for the night. But such was the act of a coward, and she deserved a knight. His words were cruel and he hated them. 'And now something for you, Mairín. When three years pass and you have not seen or received word of me, then may this seal be broken.'

She accepted the roll and bowed her head. He was glad he had been given the strength from Heaven to bequeath it to her by his own person. Then she reached around her neck and unfastened the crude wooden cross that her father had fashioned for her Confirmation. 'Since you will have no permanent mark of Christ upon your breast then I give you a humbler token to wear. You have need of remembrance of the Love borne upon the True Cross more than I at present, for its memory is burned upon my heart from sunrise to sunrise; and He is not the only presence upon which my heart reflects.'

Mairín opened his hand, placed the cross within, closed it again.

Markus dwelt upon her image as he clasped that same Cross now: the blazing in his heart spread with a quickness that threatened to consume him and leave nothing but ash upon the back of his mount. Markus's heart was a torch. He loved Mairín and it pained him like the point of a hot dagger on his heart that she had to bear the mark of his ignobility and holy disfavour.

Markus beheld the sight of true flame, just appearing in the back of a guard several feet ahead, followed by one buried in the canvas of a sack of goods behind him. Markus fell from the back of his horse, pushed the beast away, made for the nearest cover he could find: a dune of blown sand.

From there he watched the ambush unfold: mounted mercenaries carrying a Templar standard of a Red Cross across two equal bands of black and white. Such fighters were employed by leaders desiring to be covered if the assault went ill. The attacks could be "denied", passed off as having been done by a marauding band who somehow had acquired a standard of the Order. Markus found the tactic revolting: not only did it mock their ideals and principles of the Christian Knight, but its increased use told the enemy that the Order was weakening in strength. He had no doubt from whom the bandits had received their banner.

At nearly thirty strong the "Templars" were a strong challenge to the merchant caravan that was their target, but not formidable—they were not Knights, and would not have God on their side. Markus prepared to enjoin the battle in defence of the Muslims. He doubted he could save their wealth, but he sought to protect something more valuable.

Either by want or distraction, the attacking soldiers ignored Markus as he approached the chaos. He wore no device, thus his defence of the travellers would come as a shock (and, if the Saracen convoy was taken, a reason for his arrest).

The head of the first rogue—half-turned as the hands of its owner gorged the contents of a sack lying atop its now-dead carrier—encountered the pommel of his sword.

The second bandit, bearing the rank of a Templar sergeant, was more attentive having just seen a strange sight in Markus's attack upon a fellow 'Frank'. The sergeant was more heedful in his approach, but immature in his execution, and he was made unconscious.

The next mercenary to catch the eye of Markus would require a harsher rebuke: his thick beard thrust itself into the rigid feminine body that was his captive; the woman curdled a scream that pulled back the upper corner of Markus's lip. Upon reaching the preoccupied assailant, Markus channelled his disgust to his mailed boot and buried it into the scourge's torso. The man rolled off his prey and found his balance and sword with an efficiency that Markus admired—but the man was no Ridefort. He bellowed something in French that Markus took to be an insult. Using battlefield justice Markus decided this foe was better disposed of entirely: two searching thrusts, a reversed strike, two parries, another thrust, and the man was upon the ground, his blood coating the sand. Markus hoped the brigand was being compelled to prepare his soul.

The Saracens were starting to regroup and make a defence. Markus considered the present situation: the attack had come down on the convoy's right flank in a low valley; it was late in the day, which made the tactics more than prudent since the caravan needed rest. The mercenaries chose the back section of the line, a curious strategy since the most valuable of goods would be in the centre of the procession.

Markus shook off the analysis; motives were not relevant, the vile ends were the same—being murder, dishonour, theft. Markus concluded: since God had attached him to the Saracens for the present time, the safety of his guides was his only priority. After all he needed them to achieve the Sepulchre, thus it was God's will to use these unbelievers to deliver His message, given through Blessed Percy.

A figure on a white-mantled horse peaked the dune that Markus now faced; he did not descend to add his blade to the waning carnage: Ridefort—it had to be, but Markus could do nothing with this knowledge; Ridefort held the high ground and if Markus charged the Muslims may cut him down.

The Templar Master made a shout, arced his sword above his head. The attackers were reluctant to break from their aggression and needed another shout from their leader. The Saracens did not follow: one true Knight of the Temple spoke clear enough.

Markus kept his eyes on the silhouette of Ridefort; only sand lay between them, sand and the Hand of Holy God. The figure of his enemy reduced in size as he reversed his steed. Markus did not look away even after the spectre was long set beyond the horizon. It was a wonder Ridefort did not press the attack. Was the LORD denying Markus this engagement? He sheathed Audacit'in Domino and turned.

Two Saracen guards were waiting, their white garments flailing in the brief desert gale that pulled at their edges. Neither man wore an expression Markus could translate. He held out his hands in a gesture of innocent inquiry; the two men seized them, and held his arms with strength. Markus did not struggle or protest, allowing the guards to escort him to their intended destination.

When they reached the front of the caravan, Markus was dropped inhospitably to his knees; a sword came to his throat; they waited. Markus did not allow any thoughts to come to his head, save a brief prayer: *O Christ, strengthen me by your Holy Passion.*

"A sword at your throat, Frank—what comes of lost opportunities to be useful to Allah." The accented speech of his merchant host was sardonic.

"I do not fear your Death. If your sword finds my neck it is because God wills it, though I would be amused and saddened to receive my last breaths upon this spot."

The merchant was in Markus's vision now. He did not appear angry, but neither was he pleased.

"You are either the best of spies," the Muslim added, "or the worst of your kind."

"If I am the worst of Christians then it is not because I would attack my own; I would kill any man who means harm to my neighbour. As to being a spy, I have made known to you my intentions in this land. My defence of this caravan bears witness."

The merchant nodded his wrapped head

once, but Markus was not yet freed. "Your God has discarded you. But I spare you, as you may yet come to serve Allah...by your wish or not. *Subhan'Allah!*" The Muslim turned his attention back to the reforming of the caravan. With his leaving, the sword was removed and Markus's hands released in a manner that ended with his rude prostration.

"It would please you to see me grateful and acknowledge that your deity is more merciful than God. This I will not do. Faith requires long-suffering of all that occurs in our lives."

XII : the goal achieved

'The Holy City' was not very different from the seasons that Markus had occupied its buildings and walked its streets, save for the lack of Christian symbols and banners. This was the first he had seen of Jerusalem since embarking on the march that ended at Hattin. He remembered the anxiety of leaving its protective walls and the shame when he knew he could not return.

And the years that followed: every breath and sunset had brought him to this the imminent hour of divine reckoning. He did not feel any foreboding in this, save as a child who has done wrong and awaits the inevitable beating from his loving father.

The Church of the Holy Sepulchre marked the spot of the two most important physical sites in all of Christendom—the Place of the Crucifixion and the Empty Tomb of Christ. It was not a far walk from the northern gate he had just entered—the same gate through which Sir Godfrey and the Christian army had come when they liberated the city from the Fatimids. Markus knew the streets well, for both of the main gates required a person to pass the Temple Mount: where it was said Abraham had bound his son Isaac; later King David would purchase the land and erect an altar that would eventually become the location of the Temple of King Solomon, then the second Temple of Jesus' time (later destroyed by Roman General Titus less than two score after the Feast of Pentecost), then a Greek church, then the 'Mosque of the Rock', then the headquarters of the Order of the Poor Knights of the Temple—Markus's Brotherhood. And now again it was the great mosque of Islam. As Markus walked past the Mount he paused, under the pretence that the donkey he had been allowed needed the pack it was carrying adjusted. The sun was getting low and shadows added a second veil to his face, to aid the one he now wore to hide his identity from the thousands of Muslims that moved about him. He gazed at the raised site, and found the ghosts of his time there filling in his vision. Not knowing the last time the Mount had seen a Christian, he bowed, also to the Templar presence that had been there, to his mentor and brothers with whom he had served.

As he resumed his road, Markus wondered about the Church's condition. The merchant had told him of recent news: an agreement between Saladin and the Greek Emperor had been reached, which included the return of the Church. He was sure Saladin's officers had allowed no caretaker to tend the site in the years prior. Even so, Markus had been assured by his host: the doors to the Church would be unlocked and its interior would be as a Christian might expect it. In the past, this usually meant that sacred monuments and statuary (those that had survived) had hastily been returned to their prior spots; all signs of Islam were removed; any vestments and ornamentation dumped unceremoniously before the altar. It was the usual practice of the recent Muslim caliphs to tear down the Cross and turn churches into mosques after stripping them and burning their icons and adornments. However, Saladin was cunning, and likely recognized the Church of the Holy Sepulchre to be a unique prize. He had turned it into a mosque but its treasures he had preserved for bargaining pieces. Markus wondered what the Greek Emperor had given up to reclaim the site for the East.

The merchant had made clear that it would do Markus well not to tarry inside the Church for long. He was not to speak of Christ, even if it was an inquiry: he would be killed. He was not to perform rituals of prayer or reverence where he might be observed: he would be killed. Markus was to be gone from the city before the first rays of the dawn if he wanted to live.

Markus paid the warnings little heed. Only God offered a guarantee of life, and that was eternal. What burdened Markus's mind was the state of the message he was to retrieve. Percy had been an intelligent man—certainly rational enough to plan for the contingency that Jerusalem might fall and the

Christian landmarks thus left to the whims of nature. Therefore he would not have given the message to a priest, and he would not have hidden it with a mark that could easily be silenced. But Markus felt no comfort in this conclusion; it was swept away by the sight of the darkened and overgrown bastion to the Christian faith.

For the Christian, the Church of the Holy Sepulchre was Jerusalem. In decades past, the walls of the sanctuary had burned in fire and been ripped apart by Allah's fanatics, and each time rebuilt stronger and more defiant; that it stood intact at present was a monument to the Maker of heaven and earth. The Church commemorated the two most important events in a Christian's year: the Death of Christ on Cavalry and His Glorious Resurrection three days later. Although Markus had made himself ignorant of Latin, he was a religious attendee, with many of his brothers, of the Church's Paschal Triduum Mass, which was celebrated every third week of the month and not just on the annual Feasts and Vigils of Maundy Thursday, Good Friday, Holy Saturday, and Easter Sunday. In this place, during the remembrance of the Triduum, the chanting was supernal, the air intoxicating, the receiving of both the Bread and the Wine making the Holy Communion that much more special. Even as he stood in the courtyard, tying up the mule and taking a torch and Audacit'in Domino from the pack, he could hear the phantom notes of memory, smell the spice of the incense.

Markus walked around to the side and found the entrance overgrown, but the doors otherwise looking well. It served his own ends, but Saladin was known as a man of his word; therefore this Church was under his protection and the doors would need no key. Desperate to be alive again, the Prince of Audaciter-Deus pushed the door open.

Darkness met him at the threshold, but there was still an hour of the day to light much of his way beyond. He stepped into the Basilica and closed the door. There would be flint in the room where the acolytes prepared for their duties, located adjacent to the three Chapels of the Most Holy Trinity, to the left of the Aedicule—the small structure at the centre of the Rotunda Anastasis, which enclosed the Tomb.

Markus passed the Stone of Unction, where Jesus' body had been anointed after He had been removed from the Cross.

Markus stopped, and turned: behind him was a massive crucifix, with a wooden sculpture of the Christ frozen in time, his face ashen and gruesome, his eyes wet with sweat and tears, his body and limbs contorted. Delicate webs of dust hung from the circle of thorns, swayed in the breeze. Markus turned back towards the acolyte room he had settled on, but he took no step. He realised in full the hopelessness of his present. He might well need his entire lifetime to locate the message of Percy—a piece of paper with words of wisdom, perhaps even comfort. Neither would aid him: the wisdom was belated and the comfort would not delay his fate.

The Saxon prince turned a slow circle, recalling the story of Saint Peter and how an angel had guided him through prison walls to his freedom. Markus circled again…but there was no glowing messenger. He pressed on towards his original goal; found the flint where it should be, and oil, and lit the torch. For good measure he searched the drawers and cabinets for any sign of a scroll left for a Templar by a Knight of the Baptist's Hospital.

Nothing.

He crossed the transept to the antechambers and storage rooms at the right of the Aedicule: they also were barren.

Markus followed the length of western ambulatory, pausing when the light of his torch revealed an antechamber that presented itself as unkempt. He went inside and found a set of tombs inside. To the back of one of them, near the floor, was an ornate square. Markus proceeded to check out this peculiarity, which appeared to be an object set into the wall. Placing his torch into a nearby holder, Markus grasped the object and pulled it out of the recess: it was indeed a richly decorated rectangular chest, its length a bit less than half the height of Markus; upon its cover were silver and blue stripes diagonal; a scarlet cross ran the full length of the coffer; where the cross intersected was a golden circle with the Head of Christ painted upon it. Markus opened the lid, but nothing was contained inside—

although there were raised wooden sections that implied two items were intended to rest there. *Perhaps an item of cloth, with a shield over the top?* he mused. Moreover, there was something about the design on the lid... something heraldic...

The letter he had received from his father by way of the Templar Marshal: Markus had glanced it over on the voyage to Tyre, but had not the opportunity to read it—there had been a storm, and little privacy. But he had seen the prominent coat of arms painted upon the back of the roll: the gold charge of the Hand of God descending through a cloud and touching an anvil with two Fingers upon a red field. These arms of the House of Audaciter-Deus Markus knew well. But these arms had borne a new detail—an augmentation presented as a canton: silver and blue stripes diagonal, with a scarlet cross at the fore. He had secured the roll in Tyre before his departure, so he could not learn more.

Markus closed the coffer and pushed it back into place, then left the tomb.

By way of the eastern ambulatory Markus checked the gate to the Crypt of the True Cross: it was locked (and Markus knew Percy would not have risked this end). He let out a deep sigh. The night was far along now, and each hour he searched brought the danger of someone unwanted seeing the torchlight in the *Sanctum Sepulchrum*. He needed to think.

Percy had been a sagacious man, given to poeticism; each of his actions had meaning. Wherever he had placed the message in the Sacred Basilica, it was with intent and it was in a place that he believed Markus could discern.

Markus reflected back to the last time they had spoken, still clear in his mind: Percy could not replace Sir Jacques, but he did well in the effort. The Hospitaller had been the one to oversee his healing after Cresson, and become his spiritual father after Mailly's death. Their discourse on the work of Christ had often stretched long into the night. Percy had been amazed that a Templar was so articulate in matters reserved for clerics and chaplains. And although he came to love Percy as kin, Markus was too afraid to let anyone know from where he had gained such wisdom. Even so, the man posed relentless inquiries. Then one night, Percy had caught a glimpse of the Gospel of the Evangelist in Markus's possession tucked beneath Markus's robe; the Templar could not deny the man to hold it; he could not bear to ask for its immediate return when he saw the quivering lip, how reverently Percy held the Blessed Pages. The elder man had asked for some time alone to reflect upon its sacred words. Before Markus could protest, he was away from his bedside and one with Jerusalem; moreover, Markus could not read its pages in the day, with so many eyes present, nor at night when the fire-light in the hospital was kept low.

When Markus had recovered enough from his injuries at Cresson, they met every fourth day of the week, prior to vespers, to discuss the Gospel. This ritual was short-lived: three weeks later the march to intercept Saladin before he could reach Tiberius. Their final meeting had been about the LORD Jesus' healing of the blind man, who had been cured at the pool of Siloam.

There was only one 'pool' in this Church of the Resurrection: the Baptismal font in the Chapel of the Blessed Sacrament, to the right of the Aedicule—the one place he had not looked when he had searched that side of the Basilica.

Markus hurried across to the Chapel, wasted no time checking the walls—especially those the closest to the font (located at the entrance, as was tradition).

Nothing.

He leaned on the font, facing towards the sanctuary, and looked up. Above the chancel was a recessed portal covered by an iron grate—easy enough to fit a person because of the thick walls of the chapel. Markus retrieved a ladder from a nearby storeroom and climbed up to the window, which provided a view of the outside. The curtains were closed and Markus intended to keep them that way. Beside this, he had immediately spotted a sign that had made his heart leap: a small stone with a thin, faded White Cross drawn upon its face with a hasty finger. The stone could easily be grasped with a hand if bits that had been broken away were first removed, which then allowed for fingers to barely slip over. Markus worked it out; it came fast, and appeared to be broken so as to make room for small objects to be placed in the small area behind: in this case a wooden box nearly the shape of a square, and deep.

Markus held the small container and uttered a prayer of thanks, then opened the package: nothing; no token, not even a letter. He glanced back inside the open area where he had taken the stone, felt around: empty. He climbed down the ladder to the floor and looked inside the box again with his torch, turned it upside down to see if anything might fall out.

An empty box? *An empty box?!* Markus held his gaze on the flame of his torch, then looked back at the container he held. Anger fuelled by the sense of betrayal, exasperation, and worthless sorrow lit a new torch within Markus's breast. He flung the fire in his hands against the wall. The torch flashed, fell to the ground extinguished, plunging the chapel into black. He stumbled his way through the void, only the diminutive moon-glow kept him from crashing into pillars. Even so, he tripped over the base of something: it was a stair, leading up. There was a flicker at the top, like torchlight.

Markus regained a walking posture, and ascended. The climb was steep, and profound weariness came upon him. The dimness grew no brighter at the top. He turned left, found the stone face of Christ from the Cross looking down on him. From somewhere a blood-hue glow shimmered upon the sculpture's visage: the face wavered between horror and pity.

Markus cast the empty box to the floor just beneath the Crucifix marking where the LORD had been crucified on Calvary.

He joined the shattered container upon the floor. Prostrate he gazed into the stone-cut image of His Saviour: "Why do you torture your servant, O God?! You offer mercy yet leave none for your most needy of children. Perhaps your withholding is a just action.

You bring me to this place to shout the forgiveness that should be mine: if only I might be worthy.

What penance will suffice? How am I to know that I choose aright what I must do to please your Mighty Hand?

How is your bringing me here mercy?

Are empty coffers the sign I am meant to behold? Are they for my wretched body and spirit?

How is your silence compassion? Is the silence of my death necessary to free Mairín and the land of my forebears from the curse of my ill actions? Why be unmerciful to the fair creature, to my House, and keep me alive?

What work for me is there, unless you will retreat time and bring forth from the depths of Hades the days of my callow youth, my idolatrous manner at Hattin?…

You are cruel in your love and promise to cover iniquities, O LORD! Where do I have it? How do I know it?

My God, why did you inspire good Percy to call me to this Holy Sanctuary?"

"..."

"..."

"Silence.

Seasons of futility have been created for you, dear Markus; exacting nights appointed, and days of famine.

I need not ask for your divine pardon for your answer is given in your stillness: it speaks clearly, as the silence of the grave!

You know my heart and my mind, O LORD— and yet both remain under siege by my foes, as if You doubt the piety in my words!

Why speak of forgiveness, yet still allow the guilt of the sin to linger, like the broken tip of a shaft in the body?

Why cannot I have just a foretaste of the peace to come by accepting to die as I should have in that wilderness defending Your Holy Altar of Sacrifice?

Is not my unwilling spirit to protect Your Holy Cross the fullness of my iniquity—the true crest of all those sins which led to it, and have followed it— for which you hate my flesh? Then why do you not accept my sacrifice if you will not pardon my iniquity, if you will not help me in my transgression?

I pray you will do this: for I do not otherwise know for which depraved action to request Your spiritual remedy, for which other reason You have told me to journey here, for which twisted thought

You have incited dreadful visions, for which foolhardy decision You have not allowed me to enter good rest...

Here is my hand on my sword: use it to kill the enemies of Christ, or turn its blessed edges upon its imprudent master!"

"..."

"..."

"*Answer me*, Holy Father of Light!

Answer your accursed slave while he still bears the mantle of life!

It is excessive to call a faithful servant into the wilderness only to speak in silence, without so much as a rustle of the dust at my feet.

I have received the verdict of the Old Law, but not yet Your perfect justice; it is a beautiful justice earned well by me.

Truly, I did not have my life in mind when I refused Hattin, O LORD. Even so, I have fought bravely for you, O Christ, in other battles—before and since.

The wealth of which You made me steward I have given freely, and with joy, to the fair Mairín; it is an offering to You for Your grace to allow me to live and see her again.

I had hoped, by Your same gracious will, to receive the fate of a warrior-servant; I had hoped to take part in one last glory beneath Your victorious banner.

I will do a penance to you, Holy LORD, in the hope You will yet answer your humble servant: on my knees will I go back to Tyre. And if I should reach that destination—without the aid of sustenance—I will surely know You to be happy, that it is truly Your will for me to called before Your Great Throne by way of a final battle—for the glory of Your Holy Kingdom, always for Your glory: *Non nobis Domine, non nobis, sed nomini tuo da gloriam.*

Only my death shall win me back to your embrace: Is this Your will, O my King?"

"…"

"…"

"Very good: the silence of the grave is answer enough, rightly delivered so near to Your own Sepulchre.

Then I resolve to commence this course at once, before the Saracen dogs take my head and desecrate this member of Christ's body. For I would rather you spit on me in judgement than die at the hands of Allah's bloodthirsty vassals.

I shall fade as a wisp of cloud as I enter the tomb, and be known to my country, my House, no more.

Know this, O God: I do blame You not for this treatment of me, as I have not censured You for cutting off our armies for the sins of those who lead us, body and soul.

I go forth to reap the bitter harvest sown by these hands, to partake of its poisonous feast, to take many draughts from the cup of confusion: all with the hope to taste the sweet fruits of Your great mercy."

XIII : misericordia dei

Deus, Deus meus, réspice in me:
quare me dereliquîsti?
Longe a salúte mea verba delictórum meórum.
Deus meus, clamábo per diem, nec exáudies:
in nocte, et non ad insipiéntiam mihi....

The stars of the heavens danced a thousand-point ballet in perfect sync; from somewhere a caressing breeze bringing the smell of lilacs; the supernal chanting progressed further upon the twenty-second of the Psalms:

...Lîbera me de ore leónis:
et a córnibus unicórnium humilitátem meam.
Qui timétis Dóminum, laudáte eum:
univérsum semen Jacob, magnificáte eum. Annuntiábitur
Dómino generátio ventúra:
et annuntiábunt coeli justîtiam ejus.
Pópulo, qui nascétur, quem fecit Dóminus.

Matin voices; dawn bird sopranos; light more

brilliant than even those early beams which had the fortune of lighting Jerusalem spread across the landscape.

"I did not think I would taste heaven before the infernal brimstone," Markus heard himself saying; he didn't feel his lips moving.

"Or perhaps you are still in the land of the living; Tyre, to be precise."

Markus turned his head to see from where that familiar voice came. A flashing ache coursed over his crown and stopped the movement almost as quickly as it started.

When he tried again, slower, an image clarified into the solid form of a man wearing a black mantle emblazoned with the White Cross: "Charle."

"So you managed to attain the Holy Sepulchre, sir Knight."

Markus did not reply, instead moving his head back to a position where he could gaze at the farthest wall. The answer his mind forced upon him was like being given again an upsetting meal the day after it was served.

"Despite the miracle of surviving such a thoughtless quest, you are disappointed." His voice was unsurprised at his conclusion.

"There was emptiness and silence, and I still have a full conscience," said Markus; vinegar dripped from his words. "Fair wages for my noble service? I should have fallen upon my sword in that place."

"God's Voice does not come from an empty

space or in a blast of wind," Charle sighed.

"Indeed." Markus added: "We are told countless tales from pulpits of how pious souls are granted weeping statues and chattering bones—even the honey-bee serves as a vessel for Him..."

"Then perhaps for you it was meant to be parchment that speaks." Movement from the Hospitaller pulled Markus's head again: Charle had removed a small book from his robes.

Markus looked upon the small book, recognised it immediately: its creases, the places where the silver painted Cross had been worn, the spots where blood from his wounds at Cresson had stained the tops of the pages: Jacque de Mailly's copy of the Gospel as recorded by the Holy Evangelist Saint John received from the Templar Order—the same he had allowed Percy to keep until he was out of hospice. Markus had expected to see the Hospitaller again while on march, but he had not; his mind had quickly drifted from matters of the Gospel to the matters of men.

"Percy intended to return this to you. He met with me the next morning knowing there was no hope in finding you in all the mustering and that the book could not be given over to any other, lest you be dispossessed of this rare treasure. Since I was tasked to remain behind to continue my vocation to those under my care, and give aid should Saladin come upon the city, Percy gave me a roll of parchment that indicated where he had hidden the book inside the Chapel. It was his appeal that I keep it safe and return it to you; also instructions concerning how it should be returned. I made all haste, as he requested, after the army had departed."

"*Damn you!*" If Markus wished he had the strength to cuff Charle. "I came half a world for a possession you could have put in my hands upon your visit to my estate?!"

Charle rose from his chair. "Percy told me of your despondency over certain matters—both of the spirit and heart; he could not understand how a man with such a special token as the Gospel of the Evangelist of Christ—in your common language!—could be so. You were found to be ill-tempered and thankless. You did not hunger for this Book; nay, you dismissed its satiating meal as if it were nothing more than some dainty morsel of a great exotic banquet you could barely recall after a night of merry-making. You did not even ponder on the words of your fallen captain, whom you loved—who thought so much of you to pass along this blessed collection of pages. From all those he could have chosen: *you.*" The Hospitaller rose to stand behind the chair, knowing already what needed to be said next. "Markus, you carry a burden of guilt, *not* out of the will of God. You have let it partition you from all reason. It is *your* choice to condemn yourself under the penalty of the Old Law, which can no longer terrorise those who, in faith, wrap their souls in the perfect virtue: the Mantle of Christ."

"I know this Truth, Charle! Percy knew this

well, for we spoke of it. He would not send me back to this land to remind me of what I already have discerned."

Charle did not soften his gaze. "Yet knowledge does not mean faith—even the devils know and fear Christ as their LORD. Percy was implicit in his brief words to me that you *choose* to make the pilgrimage to the Empty Tomb. You knew him well enough to conclude he would not expect you to make a journey of folly. But it seems he knew you better." His voice became even again. "Percy's intent was to send your person nowhere; your broken spirit was to travel the distance, to deliberate in fervent prayer while in service to your House if not your sacred vows."

Markus closed his eyes: it did not help the raging turmoil. "It was Holy God who drew me to the Tomb, across searing desert and against enemies, where I beheld Christ on His Cross—a reminder of my failure to Him even as He has never failed me or my House. You said yourself the calling was from above."

Charle shook his head. "You twist my words. Indeed you needed to heed the calling of God. But He calls us to trust His mercy, not to make foolish treks of pride across hot desert and turbulent sea to stones no more blessed than those of one's own country. What God truly desires is a humble penitent heart, faithful to the station they have been called and the people therein."

Markus cast a raw gaze onto the far wall of the

place in which he lay; its stones were rough and edgy from decades of wear. "My heart has been on its own pilgrimage. Thus until it returns to weigh your words I am left only with the machinations of my wits and the world. When I am recovered I shall do my part to purge our religion of its perverters. I shall protect His Cross against its enemies—from within and without: this is my new oath to Him. And if God will not delight in seeing this accomplished then I cannot believe a penitent heart will quite be enough."

"And your first step upon this devil's quest, will you begin with yourself?" Charle turned away, and then turned back again. "You would pursue errant brethren when we contend with unbelievers who care only to appease Allah with our blood? Perhaps you owe our enemy a private debt, after all it was they who brought you here. No doubt your Saracen allies pray you are made whole, that your own waywardness might yet be worked to their purpose now that you have passed their trials."

Markus snapped a dangerous look to the Hospitaller, eyes that demanded an explanation.

Charle continued. "You said you were able to gain access to the Sepulchre, and that your sword was with you: No Christian is allowed into Jerusalem bearing a weapon! If your sword had been discovered, you would have been killed without hesitation. But you survived a dangerous gauntlet according to their eyes, and your hosts took careful notice of this. These men have used you; they perceive you are favoured by their god, and hope you will help them to destroy Christians. The moment you are beyond these walls their spies will know and will be upon you to beguile you, to aid you to achieve the hellish goal you seek."

Markus felt sick at the thought of being used in such a way. "Do not worry, Hospitaller. My blade will find its share of Allah's faithful, without my seeking them. Yet no one concerns themselves with those who trample the hearts of the burdened within Christendom. I will remove the tyrants, then saturate Outremer in the water of the Gospel; thereafter Rome will either swim with the tide or be dragged to the depths."

"You speak of restoring peace of spirit to your neighbour while your mind roils in graceless chaos. You will not bring peace to even the most spiritually infirm with such a message on your lips and in your actions; you bind the poor soul to the very millstone about your neck," Charle responded. "Look beyond your despair and arrogance, man! Retreat your wicked babbling, as if the Saviour had not yet come, or his declaration that 'It is finished' was deceit! All we need do is believe in Christ as the one work that pleases God. If you would save your neighbour you must first believe the promises He declares. The noon Mass will soon arrive: receive the Blessed Host into yourself for the remission of your sins, and then every day likewise for a fortnight plus one week; enter into daily confession and supplication; join me in reacquainting your mind and soul with the Holy

Truth written in this Gospel."

Markus was stunned. Truly Charle had made good use of the Book; the voice of the Hospitaller may well have been Jacques' slapping the Templar to his senses again. "You do my mentor proud, Charle, but he is dead. Each one that rises like him will be crushed by one like Guy or Ridefort. Such godless men are celebrated icons of Christendom with the beloved saints; their names draw great crowds to hear how they bathed in the blood of our enemies; their piety lasts while the red rivers flow, while the fathers of the Church sing their praises, and while men gather round them like vultures. God will not bless His Church while we abide such as these, while those like Jacques and Roger and Percy are made mute." Markus thought of the vision granted him from the Holy Grail. "Christ executed His will at Hattin, when He took His Cross from us and delivered it to the Saracen. What a damnable verdict upon us—and upon me, to whom that Cross was entrusted. It was a sign, Charle: the grace won for us upon that Tree of Shame is hidden from us; even those who were silent, or who abandoned their watches, when they should have been beacons of right-action in faith. We continue to suffer witless leaders and will not turn to more stalwart men in the manner of old. Perhaps all of Outremer is doomed to sink into the earth. That is why He has brought me back here: I will be destroyed, as I should have been with the rest of the Christian army at Hattin. I have long known this..."

...if I could but find the eternal threshold, he added to himself. Markus searched the calluses on his hands. "You must return to Europe, Charle. Return and escape the wrath to come so the people will learn from our mistake...so that those under my charge will be taught well from my idolatry."

The Hospitaller turned and crouched down on the balls of his feet so that he was eye-level with his friend. "Markus, did you ever consider that it was not the will of God for you to be at Hattin?"

"Here... in this place... the eyes of bishops and cardinals are fixed." Markus choked on the words. "Noble Saxon sons allying with Norman oppressors against a daunting foe... surely they would look favourably upon this service and speak on our behalf to King Richard and his brother..."

"But still the Saxon Houses received no audience."

Markus shook his head slowly. "But I thought—" his voice broke.

"You thought that a mighty deed would grant you a favour."

Markus made no reply or motion.

"You took on the mantle of a Templar to fight those who would enslave the world to Allah, and to win a victory for Saxon blood. Instead you are courted by Saracens, and seek out Christian prey to feed your sword..."

"They are men, like Ridefort, not Christians," Markus seethed.

"Are you the confessor of these men you hate? What prophet has told you of God's will for these men? Do you pray for their repentance with your own?"

"I pray only that the same judgment of which I am guilty be executed upon their heads, and that I may be their executioner for the evil I have witnessed from their own hand!"

Charle took in a deep breath through his nose and let it out slowly. Then he crossed his arms to make his next statement more than final. "When you are able to travel again you will be put on the first ship back across the sea, to your home."

How dare this man dictate his life, as if Markus had not the sense to carry on his own affairs—indeed did not still have a schedule of affairs that needed tending; did not have other concerns independent of the actions of a sword-arm? "Whatever my path, Charle, it is not England."

Charle lifted his brow but said nothing more as he waited.

Markus considered what he should say. He was not sure that a committed Hospitaller such as Charle would be able to understand matters of the heart. Mairín's face appeared before him; the stabbing pain in his chest and hard knot in his stomach dulled other discomforts. He longed to be with her. He imagined the soft caress of her hand upon his when she nursed him back to health and consoled his frantic wits; the touch alone was enough to retreat whatever the discomfort, but combined with her pure love was more potent than any medicine—even now though she was but the still air. A breeze swirled through a portal over his face, and Mairín took flight with it like a disturbed wisp of dust. Markus looked at Charle, and the Hospitaller nodded after a sort amount of time passed.

"In my profession I have treated many of devoted husband and pining heart. You cannot veil eyes full of love. The same depth of feeling was plain also from her upon my visit to your estate. But you are no longer a holy knight of the Church: Sir Honour is dead, remember?"

Markus was in no mood to risk having every detail of his life rebuked by a Knight of a rival Order still answerable to Roman authority. The Hospitaller's keen insight had deduced far too much; it was disconcerting. He turned his head to meet the look of Charle square. "I will rest the fortnight you have prescribed. When those days have expired, firm or infirm, I ride for Acre."

"And what is there for you Markus?"

"The end of my road, if nothing else."

"You still would speak for the Sovereign Almighty, do you?" Charle scoffed. "Your stubbornness is not only slave to a vile master but also a cunning deceiver. As it happens, the roads south are blocked to men-at-arms, this by a recent command of Lord Conrad. For should Guy fail at Acre, the Saracens will fall upon this city like locusts, and every able knight of Christ will be needed."

Markus would give Charle no indication that he had been check-mated. The Hospitaller gathered up his gloves from the table. "I am off to the midday Mass. I shall have the priest visit you."

"Let him tend to other needy mouths, or keen ears."

Charle drew himself up against these un-Christian utterances. "I am not the surrogate of your misery and unbelief. It is yours to refuse the Body of Christ, given for you, with your own lips before His sacred office. Prepare yourself, for I shall send him."

When the Knight of the Hospital was departed, Markus caught the glint of a dagger upon a nearby table. He grabbed the small blade and hurled it across the room into the doorway frame.

XIV : upon the cliff

Never did fourteen seasons of the world wax and wane slower for a man than it did for the Saxon prince and former Templar Knight, Markus of Audaciter-Deus. Bearded and forlorn, Markus stared out the small window of his quarters, as was his custom after supper. He was a condemned man awaiting the official execution sentence the divine king had not yet signed.

Markus moved his eyes over the small desk and the mangle of parchments that had collected there. One roll in particular had occupied his attention during the first months—the one written to him by his father, now with the *Ecclesia Triumphans*. The opening portion of the letter had been the hardest: the words of his father forgiving his son for making the choices he did and commending him to the grace of God with all his love; that of his mother too. After reading these words, Markus had refused to read any further until he had received Mass in deference to their charity and true fear of God; also he fasted for seven days, attended matins and vespers, and thought of nothing but their love for him and his sister.

When he had finally resumed his reading, the next details provided him by his father were 'the History of the Blessed Sword, *Audacit'in-Domino*', which Markus had now memorised: The sword had been wielded by Sir Bunian, a descendant of former Roman tribune Lucius Marcellus, and a member of the Round Table.

Before coming to Camelot, his faith had been indifferent and deedless. Through devil-work, he became indentured to a vile and rebellious master in Logres as his Grey Knight—thus an enemy of King Arthur. He was vanquished by the nephew of Arthur, Sir Gawain, in a fierce duel. Stripped of all but his robe, Bunian was sent in haste to King Arthur bearing a sealed message from Gawain to Arthur concerning Bunian's fate.

Despite severe temptations to turn aside (for surely the fate written on the message was his death), Bunian arrived at the court and presented himself. Arthur read the message, and noted that the knight had done well: for the message stated that if Bunian had arrived within a fortnight, then he was truly as fearless, God-fearing, and possessing great honour as Gawain perceived of him in the duel. Gawain further commended Bunian to the court to be a Knight at Camelot. Indeed, even as the message was read, Bunian's name appeared upon an empty place of the Round Table, where there was draped upon its seat a handsome sword with no owner. Arthur ordered

Audaciter in Domino—'Fearless in the LORD'—to be inscribed upon the sword's guard. Then it was given to Bunian upon his dubbing as a Knight under God and Arthur.

Bunian later joined the Knights upon the quest of the Holy Grail. He followed many signs and wonders all over Logres, but the Grail remained elusive. Then came news from a hermit to Bunian that Percival and two others had achieved the Grail; further, that the Holy Chalice was no longer in Logres, and neither were the three Grail Knights.

Bunian married a beautiful Lady of deep faith and they had a son. Although he defended Logres honourably, he remained heart-sick at having not achieved the Grail—believing he had failed in worthiness.

One day, he is called by the King of the Grail Castle to aid him in defending his realm. After a certain lost battle in relation to this request—in which Bunian serves faithfully but his son is killed and he blames himself for costing the King a victory—the King tells Bunian stories of the Grail, revealing his identity as none other than Sir Percival. The stories enlighten Bunian to the true worthiness of the Grail Knights: penitent humility.

Upon his death, Bunian mourns that he has come to know that he could not achieve the Grail because he believed a Grail Knight needed to aspire to be a grand moral champion. With his last breaths he confesses, "If I am worthy, it is Christ who makes me worthy: none other, and nothing else." Upon this statement, Bunian sees a blinding vision of the Grail with the Holy Trinity: the wounded Hands of Christ, being held up on either side by the Hands of the Almighty Father, while a Dove hovered in the air above His Head. Bunian is bidden to drink from the Sacred Cup. In this state his soul departs to the Lord Jesus. This vision was also seen and recorded by Bunian's loyal squire, who therefore inherited the sword and was knighted at the behest of the hermit who officiated the funeral Mass for Sir Bunian and was also his cousin.

The squire's name was Servius Plautius, and he was descended from Markus Aelius, after whom Markus had been named. But upon receiving Bunian's great sword, he took the name 'Fidem Servare' upon his dubbing, in honour of Sir Bunian, the master whom he loved. Sir Fidem and his sons continued the tradition of bequeathing Audacit'in-Domino, and it became a strong pillar upholding the House of Audaciter-Deus.

The writings of his father had nearly reached the end of the parchment. In what little space was left, he commended his son to the Church of the Virgin by Stevington; the stewards there would explain the coat of arms.

The arms would have been an amusing riddle, if he had not seen the same arms painted upon the coffer in the Church of the Holy Sepulchre. As it was, the arms were a mystery another would need to explore: his fate was tied to bloodied sand and the captured True Cross.

Until the manner of his passing to celestial shores was revealed, Markus had made himself useful to the city and its lord for the majority of the two years of his dwelling here. If he could not contend with Guy and Ridefort directly, then he would apply himself to leveraging Conrad into a position that would present his worthiness to be the next King of Jerusalem. This he had done by gaining friendships, then bringing to bear a certain number of things he had learned of the workings of his Order: the handling of money, the storing up of resources to better withstand siegecraft, the ability to be patient when attacked and observe the whole action. He rarely worked with more than one or two persons; he was moody and did not want to disturb the peace of others; he preferred to allow others to approach him for advice of their own volition.

The door to the small room opened and Charle entered, dishevelled. Markus maintained his frown and would not rise from his place in greeting. Even so, the Knight re-composed his presentation then came around his chair to look out the window.

"I see *this* is in a handsome state of disuse..." said Charle.

Markus did not need to turn. He knew Charle was holding the Gospel Testament of St. John the Evangelist, chastising him for its soiled, inert state upon the sill of the prison window. "You are beyond kind to take time from your insurmountable duties and dedicate such personal interest to how I choose to preserve my effects."

Markus heard Charle place the Book back. Then he walked back to the door where he paused before opening and half-turned his body, his face lightened with what he considered to be good news: "You are summoned by the Lord of Tyre. Arm yourself, and come!"

Markus complied; he had never been granted an audience before the ruler, and he had not sought the honour.

"The baron council has voted Conrad to be the new King of Jerusalem," Charle explained as Markus joined him in the corridor and he bolted the door shut. "He returned not three days ago with infantry from Acre and wishes your audience."

Markus stopped. The Hospitaller turned at the abrupt action of his friend. "I thought the roads from Tyre were closed to men-at-arms, Charle."

"My friend, you would not have lived long in the horrors of that siege, nor the action following at Arsuf—not in your weakened state. Moreover, making yourself a hermit in this city aided your ignorance well enough."

"'Weakened state', Charle...? This is no longer a discussion of 'hospice': you imprisoned me over two years while my chances to win back the favour of God marched out from these very gates? My body was mended by the end of that first summer!"

"Your body maybe, Markus, but your mind and spirit were still infirm—are still."

"Perhaps a bit of plague and a kiss of death would have done both of these good."

Charle's expression soured. He moved back to Markus, so that what he now said could be done in a manner less susceptible to the echo of the corridor. "You may well hear an answer to that sentiment if these testings of the Spirit do not subside. As your chaplain, I am your soul's physician. Yet it is *you* that possesses the rare cure. You stare at the vial of medicine, knowing its contents, and war against the urgency to consume its healing benefits." The Hospitaller's voice became strained beneath the oppression to hush it. "You possess for yourself the Holy Words of Christ to heal your wounded soul: a right not often granted to common men and requiring the presence of one called to the Holy Office; and you have these sacred Words in a tongue you can speak—a gift rarer still! Some certainly would press hard inquiries as to its origin, being otherwise unmarked and unaccounted, caring little for the immediate needs of one such as you. It is only by the strength of God that I am able to suppress my own burning curiosity, but I desire more your healing. Instead of reflecting on these blessings, you taunt God and make Him suffer your insolence."

"He taunts *me*, Charle! If I am forgiven of my iniquity done upon Him, then *why do I still feel its burden*, and continue to see its marks on my life? Why does He keep me in this world, taunt me like a cruel bully with love I cannot embrace?"

"The LORD God is mercy, and does not afflict us in the manner you say. But there is such a one—the devil—who observes and uses our transgression. Those trespasses and iniquities we confess are truly blotted out from the sight of God in the blood of Christ—so says the Psalmist. It is we who disbelieve and recall them in word or deed anew for the hellish fiend to torment us."

"God has kept me shackled to His commandment to put Him before all things: He set my feet upon this path, placing in my sight the memorials of my transgression; He has not granted to me the strength to complete His test of forgetting in the matter of my iniquities—for nothing else of Heaven is set before my eyes or flooded into my ears. Therefore it is clear I must accomplish severe penance in this land to His satisfaction before He will provide me the compass to return to His narrow road of absolution."

Charle blinked. "How will you know satisfaction has been accomplished?"

"Perhaps when I feel this anvil of guilt lifted from my chest so that the breath of life flows free once more—and truly I expect those to be the last of my breaths." Markus resumed walking the corridor, but Charle did not immediately follow. When the Saxon prince heard the patter of the Knight's steps he asked, "Have you any news of Ridefort?"

The answer was not quick; it was in a manner

suggesting he had not reconciled in his mind Markus's obstinate position before God and the Good News of their faith he desired to impress. "Captured, in the waning days of the first summer of the siege. He is surely dead."

"Indeed," Markus responded, putting enough weight in his voice to communicate it was the last uttered sentence that he found the most unlikely. Charle was no liar: he either did not know or (more likely) had formed his response based on the hearsay of the campaign and his own hope. There was always some truth to gossip; discerning in what element the truth could be found was the challenge. Ridefort had power and the Saracens were no fools. The latter also made a practice of parading around their superiority when it came to defeating a mighty foe. Thus ranking Templars could be assured of death: Outremer would have heard of the demise of a Master of the Order of the Temple. Therefore, he was alive and, if captured, would make every attempt to preserve his life. What could Ridefort offer his captors...?

"Gerard de Ridefort must feel my blade through his belly as the hand of execution of God's justice. I pray our LORD will grant me this one favour."

"What a fine thing it must be, for depraved men to believe they can speak for the Maker of all things, the divine Planner of Mercy and Preserver of our salvation in Christ His only-begotten Son. He has given us His Word, and men to preach the Holy Writ to our ears. It is only there that He speaks to us, and in the Blessed Sacrament if we would but heed the call to drown our ill-fated natures in Sanctified Water. The act of vengeance upon which you have set your course will see you to the father of lies. If you carry out what you desire you should truly fear that you have fallen out of the Hand of God; you will have completed becoming the god of your own fashion."

Markus continued to walk with purpose, deciding his silence and posture could better respond to the admonitions. Then Charle was suddenly beside him, grabbing Markus's arm. The action stopped them both. There was genuine concern in the Hospitaller's eyes.

"It has been *three years*, Markus," Charle said. "Saladin does not spare knights of either of our Orders. It is vain to search for him. God provides the meaning for your life." Charle squeezed Markus's arm amicably with each word: "Let Ridefort go, my friend."

But Markus had his path, and he was too long set upon it. Still, he kept his rebuke civil. "Unless your summoning me was to provide confirmation of Ridefort's demise, I shall look to my own counsel."

Charle too was set. He released Markus's arm. "I will deliver the news I came to speak. After this, I free you from my charge to indeed go and die as you your heart counsels." The Knight raised his head, addressing him as colleague but not a brother. "My tidings are that Lord Conrad requests you consider a posting in his guard, as the Templars here are under the influence of Guy. King Richard was the only voice to support Guy's claim to the throne, and there is belief the Lionheart may attempt a move against Tyre. You are the only one of your Order in this city who can be trusted to fulfil the honour to be at his side."

"So he needs a Templar Knight to cement his claim, and possibly influence other Templars? I am to defy the King of my country, who could have the holdings of my family seized for my audacity to speak for the Order against him without a command to this end? What a choice of irony: I sinned against God and a beautiful maiden to serve in this land, to preserve my family. Yet here is set before me an opportunity for the complete ruin of all things, not just my putrid existence. I have fallen low indeed in the eyes of Heaven."

"Cool your tongue, Markus. Absent your Master, Richard would not rebuke a Templar for providing objective counsel to the court of the King-elect in good faith—that is all that is asked; moreover, your King has not appealed the vote; also the Bishop backed the Lord of Tyre's election. Conrad is no pigeon, and you would be no pawn but a ranking sword in his personal guard. Conrad has twice held this mighty fortress against Saladin, and oversaw the surrender of Acre himself. There has been no stronger a ruler in Outremer since Duke Godfrey *Princeps*. Either serve the future King of Jerusalem, or go home and serve your family."

Markus let the full weight of his mind be released in his sardonic tone. "It must have been difficult for you to raise me to this high rank of self-destruction by politics."

"You speak of opportunities to please God. Here one is placed on a sparkling platter and here you scoff! A noble man of high rank at a king's court can achieve much good, and receive due protection for his House."

"The heads of noble men have also been served on sparkling platters."

Charle twisted around in disgust, a hard fist pounding the palm of his other hand with exasperation.

A shaft of guilt buried itself into his heart: he was stretching the Hospitaller too far—a Knight who had travelled a long distance to his home to honour a mutual friend, who had helped defend Audaciter-Deus against enemies not his own, who clearly had spoken well of him before a proven man soon to be King. It was unfair to make the Hospitaller carry his sorrows. Markus sighed in his mind... "Still, I am not blind to hope."

Charle faced him once more, the light of encouragement outshining the sun spilling through the small window behind him. "You will see Lord Conrad then?"

Markus let a smile break, in spite of himself. "Yes, my friend, I will see him. Perhaps God favours me yet."

"Hurrah!" Charle clasped Markus's forearms strongly, then gave him the long satchel strung over his shoulder. Inside was a new mantle bearing the Red Cross. Markus took the satchel but had no chance to place the robe upon himself, for a young squire had bounded from around a corner not far away and, being busy looking over his shoulder, nearly ploughed into the two Knights.

Charle was the first to address the youth: "What causes such reckless haste, my fellow?"

The words tumbled out of the boy: "...his majesty..." gasping; "...attacked by...!"

Markus cut Charle off, begging for more details from the breathless lad. All they received was a finger pointing in the direction of the palace and a nod. The Knights took off at a full run.

Both halted when they reached the portico of the citadel; across the way was a private chapel but Markus had spotted a friar moving at a quick pace down the colonnaded path in the other direction. "See to the Lord of Tyre," he said to Charle, checking that Audacit'in Domino was at the ready if needed. "I would detain that monk yonder and discover if he can aid us."

Charle nodded and hurried off.

Markus turned and raised a hand: "Ho there, dear servant of Mother Church: a word!" called Markus as he placed the satchel around his neck. The man did not stop and Markus decided that the monk was lost in thought. Or maybe...

He drew his sword, broke into a jog (which quickened into a run when the friar disappeared around a corner). When Markus turned the corner he saw the friar was closer and continued his run, finding it strange the monk did not think him a threat, given the present situation; indeed nothing about the man seemed very attentive, let alone startled. And in this Markus noted a discrepancy—one only a noble-born could discern: monks were hard labourers, toiling in disciplined service to God with deep earnest, even to the ruin of their bodies. Yet this friar had no limp, no hunched shoulder, no regular scratching of his skin due to the irritation of a hair-shirt—nothing about his pace gave testimony to even one painful mark or physical inconvenience. Truly, a Knight bore these in his body, but he was trained to never show such weakness to the world in the case it could raise the hope of his enemies.

Markus quickened his pace, pressing the tip of his blade firmly against the back of the man dressed in the robes of a humble 'man of God'. "You walk quick and haughty for the role you have chosen."

The Flemish accent of the voice was thick with spite: "Speak fast, for I will not entertain this posture long."

"Attempt to run and I will impale you without the honour of a defence."

"You would challenge me again?" The man turned, and added his ragged face to the condescending voice: Ridefort.

Markus tightened his grip on Audacit'in Domino, then quickly loosened it again. "God will be with me this turn."

"I refuse this challenge. I have the right to a court."

He was correct. But no court a good Christian could trust would find him guilty of anything severe, the Saxon prince decided. Indeed, Markus believed Ridefort would make *him* the subject of the trial: an unranked Knight who fled his post daring to trade words with the Master of the Temple. The Marshal who had taken him in confidence would certainly oppose him on the same principle in which he had rebuked Markus. The Templar acted swiftly, crashing the crossguard of his sword against the jaw of his captive.

Ridefort turned aside his head, his eyes never leaving Markus's face, and spit out a gob of blood. "Petulant whelp," he responded through a broken lip. "You cannot instigate me to this fight."

"You will do battle with me, or—"

"Or what, boy? You would murder a brother Christian—your own Master?"

"You are a ghost to Christendom, and therefore Master of only the shadows and hell. Moreover, I have doubts I would kill a Christian."

"*Fah!* Listen to you judge matters on which you have no authority from heaven or earth." Ridefort leaned in close. "Conrad is no friend of our Order, Sir Honour."

"You mean of Guy, who has promised much to the Templars."

"Richard backed Guy also. Would you speak against your King?"

"My liege desires to preserve his lands from Guy's rebelling. But your words are laced with hypocrisy; for what manner of respect would aid in striking down a King rightfully elected by his peers? And what ally of Richard would attack one of his subjects unjustly?"

Ridefort's eyes became slits for a moment; behind them he was surely pondering if Markus was bluffing. For his part, Markus hoped this dagger, thrown solely on the basis of the man's long reputation and his own admitted complicity in the murder of Conrad, would reveal that Ridefort was the villain behind the attack on Audaciter-Deus.

The drawn silence of the Templar Master proved the charge had struck a target. Cresson. Near-truths of selling out Christian cities to Saladin. The assassination of Conrad. Even if he was not behind the assault on the Saxon Houses (as Markus suspected), how could Ridefort suffer that his adversary possessed detailed knowledge of these and other illicit activities? He had to know that his duplicity would be judged far beyond excusable—despite his undeniable talent to make war—for the papal and Templar tribunals to stomach? Certainly the Master did not work alone; certainly there were deeper politics, connected to wealths and legacies and characters, that even the merest of revelations could lay to ruin. Ridefort was a cruel man, yet cruel men still had associates to whom they were loyal (or enslaved), warped principles to which they held truly. "I have no blade with which to run you through," said the Master severely.

Markus spotted a downward stairwell just ahead. He pushed his sword enough for its tip to indicate that Ridefort should move backward. When Markus was parallel with the stair he threw the blade down the stairs. When the clanking of the tumbling steel ceased, Markus said, "Whoever reaches it first will have the pleasure of advantage, and a free consci—"

Ridefort delivered the back of his thick elbow to the bone of Markus's cheek. He used the moments of Markus being off-guard to rid himself of the clerical habit, throwing it upon Markus with the anticipation it would disorient him, if not slow his challenger down further. It worked as well as Ridefort could have desired, due in part to Markus's white hot vengeance resulting in his flailing, causing the garment to enwrap him even more vigorously, as if working against him.

As Markus did his best to unwravel himself from the satchel, as well as the habit, and pursue Ridefort, he wondered if the LORD God wanted him to succeed. Surely God would not let the opportunity pass by: to rid His Church of such a leviathan. Markus had not been ready for Ridefort in the desert, seeking him wholly out of service to a vendetta. If Holy God did not favour his crusade of purging, what justice for the Lord of Tyre, the King-elect of Jerusalem?

Nay, Markus discerned: this was divine providence. It was clear he had been tested, like Abraham the Prophet, and found worthy of this task. Ridefort would be delivered up to him, he perceived this truth even now: the Master had come upon misfortune on the winding stair: his burly structure must have overwhelmed the last of the stone grains holding a section of the step in place. Ridefort lay face down and prone nearly at the bottom.

Seeing his enemy stirring, Markus took two stairs at a time. He braced himself against the wall to gain leverage and swung out a boot; it met the top of the Master's rising head; Ridefort spun forward with a grunt, losing whatever balance he had regained, and landed face first again on the stone landing.

The two men were in the depths of the citadel. A hewn tunnel with a deep channel of water ran past them. Up and down the channel intermittent torches, occupying stone pillars, offered the underground warren its only light.

Ridefort lunged out at Markus as he approached for a blow, catching him on the knee. It was not painful but it was effective in allowing the Master space to get to his feet. They were facing each other now, water lapping the edges of the small landing: a husky mountain of man baked by the sun versus a tightly-framed Knight with muscles and tendons tightened in self-assured righteousness.

Even before the first hard fist met his throat,

Markus perceived the brawl would go ill for him. As blow after blow, mixed with cuffs and hammer-clouts, met their marks the Knight prayed for an opening.

His heel found an object, causing him to fall back-first upon the stair: his beloved sword. Ridefort saw it also, and focused upon acquiring it immediately. Markus was relieved: dodging a sword cut meant space between the mallet-hands of the Master and himself.

The other advantage presented itself immediately: the sword was not crafted for the brawn of the Master; it was an ogre swinging a stick. The first attempt was meant only to intimidate. Markus dashed around, placing his back to the stair. Markus ducked the second swing, the top edge of the blade cutting away shards of the wall behind him, but he did not leave his position. The Master pressed his chance, raising the sword and bringing it down with a mighty swing intended to cleave Markus from collar to hip. The Knight fell off towards the ground, watching with satisfaction as the blade buried itself into the hard stone, dislodging a piece about the size of a heart. The Master tugged at the sword, but it would not be freed; it would not allow success to a defiler. Markus laid hold of the section of stair that caused the Master's initial misfortune; brought it down upon the back of Ridefort's broad neck. An unnatural cry belched from the Master, yet he held fast to the handle of the sword. Markus knew he would not get another opportunity at a close attack, thus he hurled the stone with all the might his tired limb could rally. The ragged missile glanced off the crown of Ridefort's head and into the water beyond.

Markus beheld his foe, lying half-conscious on the slab outcropping: a sacrifice upon a stone altar; beside the villain lay the ceremonial knife, which had fallen from the tunic of his adversary. Markus picked up the dagger. There was the stain of blood upon it: the blood of a Christian? One who had been chosen to be King of the Holy City, a ruler to make Outremer strong again, one to provide Markus the Templar with a station from which he could help restore Zion as a fountainhead of belief for Christendom...

"Killing me will not remove your shame, Sir Honour," rose the weak voice of Ridefort.

"Your heinous action at Cresson, and bloodlust for power, does not put you in a position to be my judge."

"I do not judge you, Sir Honour. You do that well enough yourself." There was a laboured cycle of breathing before Markus's fallen nemesis resumed. "Love is for half-wits and faith for cowards. Possess neither and you can betray neither, nor will you suffer for them. But you possess both, and your conscience has been my assassin. Your retreat from Hattin has reaped more bitter harvests than I could fathom in my hate for your surviving Cresson. You will share the eternal flames with me, of this I am c— "

There was no hesitation in the downward motion of Markus's hand, which executed his justice.

In one motion he removed the dagger just as swiftly and let it fly into the channel.

Water cleansed everything.

"The King-elect of Jerusalem is in the bounds of Heaven, Markus. We captured a Saracen spy, and another is dead. The captive accuses your King as his sponsor."

"He is wrong."

"How can you be sure?"

"Where is the weapon?"

"I do not know... I have not heard—"

"Then the bloody pagan is *wrong*, Charle."

"Then who...?"

Enemies of Christ—they do not wholly exist in the camps of Allah, Hospitaller. Markus did not intend to answer the question. Instead he inspected Audacit'in Domino. Retrieving the sword of his fathers proved difficult, resulting in a serious crack in the blade. It was nearly unusable, but there was no time for a blacksmith.

"Were you able to learn anything of the friar?"

Markus gave the Hospitaller the briefest of glances, then turned to take his leave.

The hand of Charle was on his shoulder before he could take a step. Its presence communicated apology, loss, understanding, concern: "What is your road?"

Markus did not regard Charle. "The first one I find to end my wandering."

"Take the road that leads to love and peace:

return to Audaciter-Deus, sir Knight. Please."

"Would that I deserved to travel that road, Charle. If it was meant to be mine would God have called me from that place of peace and love onto the road of perdition? I cannot enter that blessed land while I stand before our Judge with my eyes cast on the ground."

"You need only place your eyes upon the Cross, Markus: upon it the Redeemer bore our wretched flesh, fixing forsaken eyes downward for the final time. We need no longer gaze upon the cursed earth that would digest us whole, for His Precious Seal is upon us. When we stare at our feet, burdened and pitiable, Holy God, with a pierced hand and gentle, lifts up our pale faces to His own brilliant Countenance."

Markus turned now to Charle, looking upon him like a man fit for the gallows. "Your words are unwittingly inspired, and my doom is true, for I lost the Cross at Hattin." His shoulder suddenly ached, like there was a millstone in the satchel—but inside was only the tunic of the Order of the Temple. He slid the satchel off and handed it to Charle. "Present this to Richard with my devotion. I pray my King will employ its sacred weaving and stitch to more laudable use."

XV : the voice in the wilderness

Did you ever consider that it was not the will of God for you to be at Hattin?

The words of the Hospitaller distilled the whole life of Markus down to one moment in time. Could one ill decision truly have such cosmic impact? Such a notion was paralysing, and had the taint of the worst devilish trickery.

Markus often prayed for divine guidance, for a sign of what path was right. He had not expected for a golden chariot to sweep him from the field at Hattin, but surely an answer from the creation of the Almighty Father. He never knew what to expect, and the worst was silence.

The words of the Hospitaller resurfaced a dilemma: Did not his selfish choice as a boy still tether him to a duty to fulfil—to the True Cross, to his brothers? Was not discarding that duty therefore failing to trust in Providence and Justice?

What kind of miserable creature was he; to overcome one iniquity only to become ensnared again? How was it fair that snares were all about him?

"This should not be your road."

Markus stared into the crackling fire of his private camp. Beyond its perimeter of dull light, he could see nothing of the port-bound supply train, to which he had attached himself. Somewhere close his horse rested comfortably. "It is the only road to my King."

"The fate of Jaffa is not your concern."

Markus rubbed his neck, doing his best to dispel the feeling of a searing blade having touched him. "I will have no other purpose, save to destroy any soul foolish enough to waylay my course."

A figure, terrifying in its beauty, emerged from the pitch of night like a wraith. The Pure Light tracing the folds of his white cloak was like that of a white-blue star; the hood and shadows obscured the man's appearance save the shimmering eyes. In one hand a sword was drawn, but presently lowered. *"Your road is to your homeland of green hills and fluttering hearts."* The voice sounded like three and three thousand, echoing off a range of mountains and caverns despite the camp Markus being located in the flat wilderness of sand to all horizons.

"None, save Holy God, have the ability to call me to that path."

"Do you know His Voice?"

"The words would be telling."

"Do you know His Words? For indeed He speaks them to you; Words outside your mortal cloister and private judgment hall."

Markus found his hand drawn to a small bulge against his chest—the place where the Gospel testament given him by his former captain was secured. A buried memory of Jacques came into his mind, vivid—as if it had only taken place that day; the Templar Commander had been teaching his Knights to believe only in the Word of God: 'it is the old deceiver who comes in voices sounding like our own—familiar, affirming of our wayward desires and visions.'

But Jacques spoke also of duty and fulfilling one's promises, had he not? Jaffa lay at the end of this road, and it was there that he would finish his obligation to Christendom, as he should have done at Hattin. "You are a fool to challenge one intent on retrieving the favour of his God."

The anonymous figure might have been considering his naked response in his silence, but Markus felt that his thoughts had been laid equally bare when the answer came: *"Draw your sword, Knight, and let the fool be revealed."*

Markus did so.

The duel seemed to stretch hours. Every thrust, parried. Every cut, blocked. Every trick, countered. It was cold enough for him to see his breath and yet Markus was soaked to the bone with perspiration. Markus's opponent ducked his favourite reverse attack and touched the shoulder of his sword-arm. The pain was instant, the contest was ended.

Dropping to his knees, Markus coughed and

gagged as he sucked in breaths.

"Valiant men seek to avenge sanctuaries of stone and wood, even courting death," the stranger's voice said, piercing the air with atypical clarity. *"And all the while they pay no heed to steadfastly guard the true holy places where the Kingdom of God dwells."*

Markus was cut to the heart. "I lament I am not among the valiant or the steadfast. But I aim to right this iniquity and take hold of my salvation."

"Your depraved mind—a tool of that liar and murderer from the beginning—prevents you from discerning your grievous trespass was not at Hattin nor as a youth, but in continuing to reject the Incarnate Love; and you despise any creature through whom God would work to pronounce this Love. Repent."

"How can I receive such a gift while the oath to Holy God before my Order lays in ruins, unfulfilled."

The cloaked man bent down so that his eyes were not a hand away: *"All has been fulfilled on the Mount of the Skull, for you. You remain hardened against the forgiveness purchased for you, given you in the Blood of the Blessed Eucharist. You choose idolatry, desiring to be 'messiah' to yourself in this land. Repent."*

Markus shook his head. "The fulfilment of which you speak cannot be. I would feel this if it were so!"

"You were shown the Most Sacred Chalice, Markus. Did you think the miracle of this vision was meant only for Christendom? You were invited to cast your eyes into the Grail. The Cup is for you: either drink of its Mercy provided through faith, or become drunk on its Judgment by your stubborn unbelief." The figure straightened. *"Repent: the time of your reckoning is upon you."*

Markus bent forward, the crown of his head touching the sand. The sound of hooves turned his head, where he saw the stranger sheathing his sword and then mounting a magnificent waxen steed.

"Follow your road, or follow mine."

The cloaked figure patted the head of the horse as it carried its rider forward, to the north—away from Jaffa; even before both were beyond the circle of firelight, they were hidden from the eyes of Markus, as if a veil had dropped over them from beyond the night.

XVI : the struggle of jaffa

The last full month of the fifth summer after Hattin was nearly upon all the land. Added to the blazing furnace of the sun was the white-hot fire of men intent on preservation or reclamation.

By the Feast of the Circumcision of Christ, King Richard had moved on from Jerusalem, recognising that, if taken (and there was good reason for the confidence this end would have been mere formality), the great city could not be long held by his dwindling army. Thus he refortified crucial Ascalon by spring; he ordered Acre prepared for a siege, where rumour spoke excitedly of the True Cross being located there. In consideration of this or not, Saladin took the opportunity of Richard's distraction to turn his swords loose on Jaffa: Acre was too much to hope for, and his being routed at Arsuf a year prior was nearly a loss too much for the caliphate. The 'Justice of Allah' needed strengthening of its own, and that required a conquest of value if Saladin was to convince the emirs to continue their support.

Markus was near the end of his writing on a

scroll as the third day of battle commenced its fourth hour outside his window of the citadel; orange bands from the late afternoon sun stretched upon the walls.

For the Saracens, Jaffa was ideal. It was direct on the sea and therefore a logistical key in any initiatives towards Jerusalem. Furthermore, the town had become rich in produce and poor in battle readiness. That Saladin had destroyed Ascalon on a previous occasion, even while acknowledging its beauty and wealth, had no apparent impact on the present rulers of Jaffa. The Sultan of Egypt was surely confident that with the modest settlement controlled the 'Franks' would court no thoughts towards Jerusalem whilst he recomposed himself, and reassured his own kingdom.

Notwithstanding its lax reputation, the garrison was presenting an unyielding and gallant resistance, leaving Saladin with little more than the dust gathering upon his tent. Even so, Markus hoped the Lionheart would join them in all haste, for the sake of the city that had done well by him for the better part of a fortnight. The full result of this day could not yet be discerned, but the wall defences vowed permanent cracks well before dusk if there was not relief soon.

Markus sealed the scroll on which he had been writing, tied a red ribbon about the centre, and placed it against the skin of his hip. He took another appraisal of the battle through the thin portal: an ominous tremor rippled beneath his feet; men shouted desperately and moved out of sight.

A breach. Somewhere close by the arduous work of Saracen sappers had yielded its dividend: a broken wall, perhaps even an entire collapsed rampart. Judging the way Jaffa's guards continued to move to that area, thereby risking other vital areas of the battlements, Markus concluded the situation was dire.

There was further movement, sneaking and more curious, just below his line of vision. Markus strained to see, pressing his face against the stones to the point that he could feel the rough surface denting his skin: it appeared like a small detachment of Saladin's bowmen, who must have scaled a wall no longer defended; they were spreading themselves upon the upper portion of a stairway and its landing. A shaft was launched by one of the invaders out of sight, then several more. From their position they could pick off Christian defenders.

Markus hurriedly dressed for battle. The corridor passing by his door would lead him straight to that stair.

He picked up Audacit'in-Domino, now repaired and strong, and sheathed the sword. Beneath lay the letter written to him by his dear father. He wrapped the parchment around the scroll inside his tunic, tying a strip of leather around so they both would remain together in their place.

The last token remaining was the Cross pendant given to him by Mairín. He stroked the wooden edges: the loss of the sacred relic of the True

Cross—his prior charge—wrenched his heart anew, fair judgment for breaking pilgrim tradition and not leaving the ornament at the Holy Sepulchre; Mairín entered the sight of his mind, an exemplary tree of Christian charity and faithfulness—a tree Markus believed forbidden. He placed the token about his neck, and stepped out the door.

"Markus! *Deo gratias*...!"

He turned to the sound of a familiar voice, one he had not expected nor was sure he welcomed. "Charle..."

The Hospitaller completed the distance that had separated them and embraced his fellow.

"How did you find me?" Markus inquired.

"Through Providence, and none other way. Richard learned of your plight here, and sailed from Acre. I rode with a column of men, and when they were detained at Caesara I pressed on to—by the grace of God—bring tidings to this good city that Richard is nigh." Charle took a breath, and now regarded Markus sombrely. "Truth be told: I had hoped you would have long ago made use of the port here."

Markus ignored the last implication. "My King is not likely to find much to save by the time of his arrival. The wall is breached, just now; we will be overrun by nightfall."

"The garrison can hold within this citadel for a night," Charle countered. "Hope is not yet spent."

"We do not know the will of Heaven in this hour."

"No, Markus, we do not. These hours call for endurance and not vain-glory."

Markus kept his silence. Yet he doubted he could fully shield the intent in his eyes.

And the Hospitaller confirmed it. "What are you planning, Markus?"

"Come." Markus proceeded down the passage where it opened upon a path on the rampart. He peeked around the corner: two Saracen bowmen, and a third partly hidden could be seen. Markus indicated with his fingers that there were more, and in what action they were presently engaged.

Charle understood what needed to be done and pulled Markus back to a safe distance again. "I will get some men and horses," he said in a small voice. "We can drive these fiends from their perch with ease."

Markus shook his head. "I agree these must be located, but not for a task such as can be handled by a lone sword; every moment we tarry, another Christian defender is robbed of life. Make your way to the houses and help prepare families for the sacking that is soon to come. Let the honour of none be spoiled, nor for their children or what possessions they deem most necessary to be taken."

Charle understood the wisdom in Markus's words but he also had clear concern that the soul of his friend was on the brink of ruin. "You cannot take the number of archers of which you speak with your sword alone."

Markus let out a deep sigh, but he was resolved to engage the archers without aid. He took several steps back towards the enemies.

"Your actions will lead to self-inflicted death, Markus!" warned the Hospitaller, following behind. "This will be written against you!"

"I am meant to die in this land, Charle," Markus countered. "Let me meet this fate and take some of these foul heathen with me for the glory of God. Look at them..." Markus pulled Charle to view the bowmen: unaware they were being measured, they took their time to line up their targets with freedom—revelling in their wealth of time, happy to attribute their position to Allah as a blessing and proof of the superiority of their false belief over the one true God and His children.

Charle turned, with force, his fellow Knight to look at him. "Now view the man God has sent to reason with you!"

"The old deceiver caused even Blessed Saint Peter to attempt to prevent the death of our LORD Jesus."

Charle bristled. "Yes, the deceiver is here. If you maintain your intent, you will learn soon enough in whose ear he was whispering."

"This is what God wills for me, Charle..."

"No, the course in your eyes is what *you* desire for *yourself*, because you are blind with guilt, pride, and a want to usurp the LORD's governance over you. You believe you choose a path of glory, but it is a path of destruction and no work that will please Heaven."

Markus looked at Charle, and then at the hand of the Hospitaller that was holding him in place. His fellow had spoken true: Markus's conceit was discovered, made a target, and a shaft placed clear through.

Markus removed his belt, with sword in its place, and handed it out to Charle. The Knight of the White Cross hesitated, unsure of the aim or genuineness of Markus's action. With tentative movement, the Hospitaller freed his hand from its grip, placing it on the scabbard. When this was done, Markus dragged his fingers to the exposed grip and unsheathed the weapon.

Markus's charge into the Saracens had the full advantage of surprise. Charle retreated into the passage, stunned in equal measure, refusing to bear witness to the end.

XVII : a third duel of wills

Jaffa was overrun. What was left of the garrison had retreated into the citadel as the town was sacked, allegedly with the guarantee from one of Saladin's agents that all lives would be spared.

Charle did not remain with the defenders. He needed to go house to house tending the wounded left behind by the ravaging swords, lending his blade to those protecting heirlooms, wives, and daughters from looters and those looking to make a profit in unspoiled captives.

Some hours into the night, word had come to his warriors from Saladin himself to disperse. Charle remembered well the Sultan of half a decade before who thought nothing of employing the standard expectations of war to their fullest extent, often personally. Therefore Saladin's leniency was telling: he was unsure of his rival, Richard the Lionheart; the Saracens were running thin on resources; the pressure from the caliphate was exacting its toll; there was Jerusalem to preserve above all. Saladin wanted Jaffa secured in haste and without further delay, even if that meant protecting Franks—just so long as the Christians were out and duly subjugated. Charle, watching nearly fifty knights and their families gather at the south gate, wondered just how close Christendom might be to pushing their enemies from Outremer altogether.

Then came the cry from the sea: *Christ le Seigneur, et Cœur de Lion!*

The Saracens, outnumbering their foe at least thirty for every one Christian sword, were set upon by Richard himself; arrow shafts rained upon Allah's faithful by the thousands, wave after wave.

In less time than a watch of the night, Saladin was routed as he had been at Arsuf.

There had been no pursuit. For all his prowess and courage, the King of England had given all that could be given on this night. And the Muslim force would not yield the city they had just invested three days acquiring. They would regroup and try again. Richard needed his small force to be ready, and rested.

For now there was time to gather the wounded, bury the dead. In the bright moonlight Charle stepped across the lifeless field on his way towards one rampart, looking for a body in particular to bury.

And finding that body.

The Hospitaller rolled off four dead Saracen bowmen. Beneath was Markus the Saxon prince. Nearby was Audacit'in Domino, which Charle retrieved. The Knight regarded the Templar, a life tortured by burdens of the soul—weights that he would not see removed save by folly. But he was a fellow brother of the Holy Orders, and a lord who strived for liberty on behalf of his neighbors, under God. He moved a wayward lock of hair, stiffened with dry blood, from the forehead of the man whose spirit he had hoped to give peace. Charle caught sight of the wooden token of the Christian faith, it too covered in blood—

—*still* wet *as if from an open wound!*

The Hospitaller tilted his head so his eyes were level with Markus's body at the neck. And in the moonlight Charle perceived what he had not dared hope, albeit the faintest sign: life!

The sum of injuries upon the Lord of Audaciter-Deus had challenged every skill and discipline the Knight of the White Cross possessed. If it was not for his being spelled by Balian, the Lord of Ibelin, the Hospitaller was sure he would have failed as friend and physician. At first Charle had not allowed Balian to take up Markus as his charge; surely such a ranking nobleman had more vital matters to handle, such as working out an accord with Richard that Saladin would accept. Even so, Balian insisted, bringing supplies from his own tent to refresh those exhausted, and even his private altar.

Charle was taken aback at such charity towards an anonymous soldier the Master of Ibelin surely could not have known.

Balian responded with a great tale: In the

early spring of the same year as Hattin and the fall of Jerusalem, he had been part of a prestigious delegation on behalf of the Holy City to settle the matter of the treachery of Raymond of Tiberias against the Christian kingdom. The delegation included both Masters of the Orders, as well as brothers under their command. Balian had been detained a day at his house in Nablus for business, and so the delegation rode ahead, intending to meet up again at the fortress at La Fève. After celebrating Mass for the Feast of St. Phillip and St. James, Balian had arrived at the castle—to find a camp, wholly unoccupied. Bewildered, the Lord of Ibelin and his squire resumed their road, coming upon a Templar gravely injured across the chest. After tending his injury the Knight provided his name—Honour—and told them of the maddening disaster at Cresson.

When he was well enough, the Templar moved on to Jerusalem. They met again during the march to meet Saladin at Tiberius, where the wife of Count Raymond was in peril, where Balian learned the Templar's true name was 'Markus' and was the son of a Saxon lord. A friendship took root between equals.

Raymond had since repented of his treason. Whether his contrition was true or nay, the Count presented a good case to dig in at Sephora, and deny Saladin the choice of ground—even if it meant the loss of his city and wife, Acre and Jerusalem could not be compromised. Balian was impressed with Markus's articulate fortitude against King Guy and the Master of the Temple, Gerard de Ridefort, in supporting Raymond. Alas, the Master toyed with Guy's flailing reputation, and the army was commanded forward, where they met their cruel fate at Hattin.

Balian survived on his good repute among the Sultan and his emirs, and intended to immediately retreat to Nablus; he found no trace of Markus among the row of piked Templar heads, nor anywhere else— and he could not tarry to look.

Yet on his way to Nablus he happened upon a sight: Markus, lying face down in the desert sands, ill from exposure and distraught. He took the prince of Audaciter-Deus to his home. But Saladin would soon be there with his army. So he charged one of his most trusted knights with seeing Markus to the hospitals in Thuringia—a Frankish realm Markus had spoken of during their conversations for reasons the Saxon prince had not made known.

Charle filled in the story from there: Markus had indeed made it back to his estate, yet he had returned to the Land of Christ out of guilt, where he believed himself called to answer for his abandoning his task of defending the True Cross at Hattin— having chosen the love of a woman whose heart he had ignobly slain as a brash prince.

The Lord of Ibelin was moved by these details, and agreed that Markus had placed himself in a difficult position, lamenting how the devil strove to rob *all* of the Blessed Cross.

Following the anointing of Markus, in

preparation of the final rites, Balian joined his priest and Charle in a prayer of mercy and preservation, that Markus might be restored if it be the will of God. Then he took his leave, to provide aid in matters of politics that grew more ominous by the hour. By his desire, his priest would remain indefinitely.

It was the third night. Markus stirred.

Somber mumbling jolted Charle awake. The priest prepared for confession and to administer the Eucharistic provision.

"Do not try to move, my friend," said Charle, gently placing a stabilizing hand upon his friend. "You required enough sewing that you could pass as a worn blanket."

Markus's eyes responded to his voice in a languid and searching manner.

Charle imagined that the Saxon prince was surprised that he was still for this world. "Yes, God wishes life, for at least a bit more time. Your wounds are grave—He may yet take you before the rising sun." He looked to the priest, who was ready, and leaned close. "Have you any confession, sir Knight?"

After several attempts, Markus answered with a difficult rasping and intermittent loss of breath: "I cannot escape the sin of Hattin …Charle. …I have confessed this…iniquity…to God on nights more numerous than the stars. …its weight remains… bolted to my spirit. Sin cannot be washed from this corpse. My honourable death was…at Hattin… protecting the Cross of Christ. …have lived beyond the years …allowed me."

"Hattin was not your calling, Markus," Charle urged. "Surely, when Ridefort heard you had survived at Cresson, he assigned you a charge he expected you would not survive."

Markus shook his head once. "…no reason to abandon our LORD's Cross to those who hate Him. I ran… …afraid to die…before I could love. La— Lady Mairín… She came to love me …love that drove me, in part, to my vows. That we came to be reunited… … only from God. I perceived He wanted our love as… sacrifice for my seeking battles for which I had not been created, for my rebellion against my good father. But He wants more: He wants…*everything*!" The Knight looked to Charle, eyes glistening with frustration, ache, *sehnsucht*, penitence: "God has forsaken me, as I forsook Him. He has rightly stripped me of all dignity, yet He allows me…to die in the presence of a…frie— … faithful companion. You are a monument to men."

Charle wanted to interject, to softly rebuke his friend for an unwarranted acclamation.

Markus continued: "The manner of the passing…of my possessions…can be found in the scroll that…God-willing, you have discovered in your treatment of…my person." Markus touched the arm of Charle with the back of his hand, but to the Hospitaller it was as if his friend had gripped him in the strength of brotherhood. "Promise me… …Mairín must not fill her heart with anger towards Heaven for what I… I have wrought in my transgression."

Markus closed his eyes. The priest produced a Sacred Host from his rotund pyx, and then a small decanter, both of silver. He opened the vessel and poured a minimum amount of Sanctified Wine into a miniature silver spoon—

"The Hallowed Graal, my LORD? for me...?" Markus exclaimed as streams cascaded over his temples.

The priest looked briefly to Charle, who shook his head, having no idea to what fantasy Markus was referring.

The priest dipped the Host into the Wine; held the Blessed Sacrament aloft, chanting the opening verses of the sixty-seventh Psalm of David.

The priest looked upon the dying Knight with deep pity, absolved him of his sins, and indicated to Charle he was ready to administer the Holy Sacrament.

Charle managed to push Markus's jaw down enough for the Host to be placed on his tongue. When this was done the priest held up a Crucifix in the palm of his hand and gave the Blessing of Divine Provision, praying that Christ Jesus would protect the soul of the Knight and lead him to eternal life. The priest made the sign of the Cross over Markus, then Charle, then himself, genuflected, and then proceeded out of the tent, remaining outside and chanting in rich, low tones with such deep mystical beauty that the Hospitaller was unable at first to speak through the emotion that welled up from his heart.

But as he watched the shallow breaths of his

fellow Knight, barely perceptive, he gripped Markus's blade, Audacit'in-Domino, and began: "You have confessed your heart, dear Knight; you received the Blessed Body of Christ, given to reconcile the world, and the Blood of Christ, shed for your sins, which were made His own upon His singular Holy Baptism. And now, before you commit yourself to your final battle, I pray you will hear me.

"God was with the Lionheart, for he turned the tide: Jaffa was not taken. There is talk that Saladin will come to terms, open all of Jerusalem and her holy places for Christians to preserve and visit, unmolested and without tax. Your service had aided in this end, dear Knight, and is worthy of remembrance." Markus gave no indication the words had entered his comprehension. Charle allowed a terse, weak smile—a façade for feelings pressing against his throat like a river about to break its walls.

"By His grace, God has used your imprudent journey to this land for good, that you might see the proof of His unchanging love in The Sepulchre, where your sins and mine have been buried from the sight of Holy God for ever. Though that Tomb was given the dead body of our LORD, it was quickened again and the Tomb could not stomach Him. Thus we too, when this earth passes away, shall rise from our tombs as did our LORD from The Sepulcher. Every church in the world, most especially when the faithful gather around the Great Liturgy of the Word Incarnate with the *Ecclesia Triumphans*, is the testimony of His necessary death and blessed Resurrection: a witness to the unyielding desire of God to make us His perfect vessels. In the Divine Light of this truth God inspires men to a fruitful life of service that pleases Him, for the sake of Christ. The curse of sin causes us to stumble, yet His love is steadfast, Markus, and His mercy abundant, even though we cannot comprehend His work this side of Heaven.

"Do you hear me, Markus? He restores to us joy we rightly feel we do not deserve, but must still receive. You have made poor decisions; as do all this side of Paradise; repent, pray for better discernment; live! "

Charle could no longer detect the rise and fall of breath in Markus. He placed his ear against the chest of the Knight and felt rather than heard the faintest of *thumps*. The Hospitaller suddenly felt desperate: "Our LORD is speaking to you in this moment, dear brother! …You fight a battle already won for us. …You cannot allow yourself to go before the Judgment Throne devoid of His mercy. …Do you hear my words?"

Charle wiped a trembling hand over his face, spotted the Gospel Book that Markus's captain had bequeathed to his young protégé. Charle took it up and placed it upon the Knight's chest, his hand remaining upon its cover: "You still have a most important task given you…! Others must receive these Words. For this you were meant to *live*, Markus! In His gracious mercy, God sheltered you at Hattin, and the Angel of Death passed over—but the evil one still hopes to destroy you there! An ignorant death will be his terrible victory! Markus…!"

There was not a sound, save that of the priest, still chanting his inspired supplications. Frustrated, and hateful of the murderous foe, water gathered, washing Markus from the vision of the Hospitaller. "Please, dear LORD of all compassion," he croaked, "open his ears and grant him some breaths to ponder!"

"You are not forsaken, dear brother! You are not! Christ bore this—" Charle's voice broke, and he wept.

epilogue

The late morning sun was nearly obscured by the oncoming thunderclouds—the first such storm of the new spring. Beams of light from the heavens pierced the dark covering, cascading to the earth and brightening the waking grass to an epiphany green. Then, calmly, the beams faded behind the billowing clouds, waiting for the storm to weaken and be chased along by their source.

Mairín sat at the window of her cottage on the estate of Audaciter-Deus, watching the storm play across the tor. The silhouette of another horse and rider peaked one of the lesser crests on the distant horizon. It was the fifth one since the equinox, but the first in nearly a fortnight. The winter had been harsh and the vassals needed food and wood. These folk were more to Audaciter-Deus than mere fiefs: they were brothers and sisters of the same Body; as much family as any who were blood of the line. Thus Lady Dawnlyn was generous, going without portions for her own house, as her mother and father had when they kept the estate and harsher days descended.

Mairín looked at the open scroll on a small table beside her—a parchment she had read enough times to fill a month of days; the one given her by Markus before his leaving. By now most of its words were written upon her mind:

my dearest mairín. if you are reading my hand the three years have expired. the journey i was called to make had only two paths: the one back to you or the one that is eternal. hope is a fine thing, and i would steal it from no one. do not hope for my return. when the rider tops the hill to bring you the confirmation your heart will need, pray continue on in the blessed son of god with most precious gift of earthly life, given by the almighty father and preserved by his righteous spirit.

as sir honour i could not love you, and by his transgression i came to know i would not have that chance. for neither feigned ignorance nor a new name can hide a man from true judgment. hate me fully in this. it is not the fault of our creator when his creations choose to be witless. there is nothing on this earth or in the great expanse more good, more just, or more wise and loving than the lord god. i know this to be so...

The rider she had seen dismounted, deciding to walk his horse to the gate—it was a sight reminiscent of the Hospitaller's arrival years ago. Was this chance?

Mairín fought a downpour of tears from the gale of harsh disappointment. She moved to stand just outside the threshold of her small abode, where the fragrant air could enter her body as a type of bitters. The storm was beginning to pass.

Mairín moved over to a small holly tree. It appeared fit for death, but under Mairín's tending, patient hand it was surviving—indeed new blossoms were emerging upon some of its branches.

My dear Markus requested of me not to hold the manner of his suffering against You, LORD God... Will You permit a woman her time of grief and anger? Will You permit that what Markus discerned as Just and True may not be so for others?

Mairín closed her eyes, steadying herself on the tree as another swelling tide of emotion threatened to destroy her composure. She played with one of the ivy leaves upon a branch that had come to wrap itself around the trunk. The ivy had been a welcome comfort as she had tended the stricken tree over the many seasons, reminding her that there was life even where death desired to have its way.

I am confident, Holy God, that I will come to be grateful to have known our Markus for the years I was allowed than for none at all. The ache that I could not turn his pain to love will remain, but it will not turn to the hating of You, O LORD, Designer of Salvation. I shall pray for a strong hope in Your promise of preservation, that I might see again my dear Markus upon that Landscape forever illuminated by Your Eternal Present–where the past cannot torture, nor the future deceive.

Mairín looked upward: the clouds were no longer there; the azure sky was waiting to be lit again by the day-star.

Dearest LORD: I wish it were Your good will that I could know if Markus received what he needed in the place of Christ's earthly life. I am prepared for that answer to be revealed with the passage of time, if you deem me worthy of the knowing. The walk of our faith is ever dipping into shadowlands. But–for those who cling to Your Beloved Son–we are given rest beside still waters. O to hear from the rider that Markus grasped to his Saviour to the bone...

Mairín, turned her eyes back to the holly tree. She followed the ivy branch from its ground source until it ended around the upper part, where a growth of mistletoe hung above her head. She reached to break off a sprig, barely noticing the swift passing of a villager.

Then another flew by.

Then a small group, which succeeded in interrupting her plucking the mistletoe branch. She took up the hem of her dress and added wary steps to those of the folks who were running to the gate.

The sun broke out from the clouds, bathing the whole landscape in supernal glow and warmth.

No; the people were not running to the gate, but through it, to the rider she had seen dismounting, who was now halfway across the meadow. He did not wear the black mantle and tunic of a Hospitaller, yet he did exude the stoic bearing of a Knight weighed by the spiritual and physical scars of his vocation: his face was still unrecognisable from where she stood but his posture was familiar.

Mairín spotted Lady Dawnlyn among the throng, heard them all joyfully shouting together as they embraced the Knight: "*Numquam desperate, confidite deo!*": 'Never despair, trust in God!' Bells tolled from the chapel, rolling across the blessed landscape.

The Knight removed the hood and thus also the shadows veiling his face. The Lord of Audaciter-Deus saw her. He wore a fine velvet robe of white with embedded lace in the cuffs and along the hem, a black 'Cross patonce' outlined in gold was stitched over his heart; enclosing his body was a hooded cloak of white sheepskin, of a kind fashioned for a prince; the eyes of Markus reflected the joy of a spirit renewed in the flood of salvation, even as his face was solemn with maturity. He greeted her by holding high the Cross she had given him.

Mairín moved fast now. The waters of joy could not be held back.

They fell into an embrace, and all the village with them.

There would be other battles, more trials, again iniquitous failures. Yet to such as these, who abide and endure in Sacred Communion with Holy God, are promised the overcoming on the Day of the LORD, for the sake of Jesus Christ.

✠

O Christ, sanctify me with Thy Spirit.

O Christ, save me by the bread of
                                    Thy Body.

O Christ, give me life by the wine of
                                    Thy Blood.

O Christ, wash me clean by the water
                                flowing from Thy Side.

O Christ, strengthen me by Thy Passion.

O Jesus, Holy King and Our Portion in
   the land of the living, hear my prayer:

Hide me within Thy Wounds,
   and keep Thou close to me;
defend me from the evil enemy.

At the hour of death, call me before
   the Throne of GOD,
      that I may praise the LORD with
         the fellowship of Thy saints,
            Forever and ever.

based on the 'ANIMA CHRISTI' PRAYER

.

Author's Note, on the word *crusade*

The word *crusade* did not exist when "crusading" took place, starting in 1096. So why did I choose to name this story of Markus the Templar, 'Crusade'.

According to the Oxford Dictionary, the word *crusade* was first written down in the 18th century. It was linked to the West's military campaigns of the High and Late Middle Ages with explicit religious contexts and papal support by Christian Arabs in the 19th century (who were translating French history into their language and did not have a better term). Almost immediately, it was (and is) ill-treated or mis-used by other parties, either as part of anti-Christian propaganda or as synonymous with "a cause" or "a movement" within political or cultural contexts.

The word traces back to the 16th century French *croisade*, and was influenced a century later by the Spanish *cruzado*.

But the word has its roots in the earliest Latin and French, *crux* and *croisee* respectively: "cross". Literally translated, *croisade* means "the state of being marked with the cross", in reference to the kings, knights, and soldiers stitching crosses on their tunics or cloaks, pledging themselves to the 'armed pilgrimage'.

A fair argument is made that Christendom was right to contend with the aggressive imperialist goals of the Muslim world, alone based on precedent from the facts of the 7th through 9th centuries. Even so, hindsight through the lens of the Reformation makes the improper witness towards Christ, not to mention the egregious theology, connected to such overt and Church-sanctioned calls-to-arms very clear to us. The vocation of 'the sword' lies exclusively with the nations (Rom. 13:1-7).

What are Christians to make of this word, *crusade*? Beginning with our Baptisms, we have the Name of God placed upon us; during the Divine Service of Holy Baptism pastors will usually make the sign of the *croisee* upon the forehead and heart of the one being Baptized. Therefore, by its literal definition, all Christians are engaged with the world in *croisade* —"the state of being marked with the cross".

However, it is revealed in the Word, truly, that to be in *crusade* does *not* mean Christians making war with military forces over religious doctrine or for lands that we perceive to have religious importance (cf. John 4:19-24). Through Baptism, Christians are in *crusade* daily in the spiritual realm, as Jesus makes clear through St. Paul in his epistles to the Romans (6-8) and Ephesians (6:11-12ff).

Stitched Crosses: Crusade is a story of Christians Baptized into Christ, and all the struggles that are connected to the reality of *croisade*. Indeed, as the story presents: Baptized into Christ or no, belief or unbelief—all humanity wars in spiritual campaigns beneath the Cross where reconciliation with God has been purchased for all (Romans 1:18ff).